UNCHARTED WATERS

A RAVENWOOD MYSTERY NOVELLA

SABRINA FLYNN

A Ravenwood Mystery Novella

SABRINA FLYNN

UNCHARTED WATERS is a work of fiction. Names, characters, places, and incidents are either the product of the author's overactive imagination or are chimerical delusions of a tired mind. Any resemblance to actual persons, living or dead, events, or locales is entirely due to the reader's wild imagination (that's you).

Published by Ink & Sea Publishing

www.sabrinaflynn.com

ISBN 978-1-955207-12-6

eBook ISBN 978-1-955207-13-3

Cover Design by MerryBookRound

www.merrybookround.com

ALSO BY SABRINA FLYNN

Ravenwood Mysteries

From the Ashes

A Bitter Draught

Record of Blood

Conspiracy of Silence

The Devil's Teeth

Uncharted Waters

Where Cowards Tread

Beyond the Pale

Legends of Fyrsta

Untold Tales

A Thread in the Tangle

King's Folly

The Broken God

Bedlam

Windwalker

www.sabrinaflynn.com

FOREWORD

Dear readers,

Fair warning: This novella does not contain a mystery. I've always found it unrealistic for private investigators or amateur detectives to constantly be tripping over bodies wherever they go. One starts to wonder if the detective isn't really the murderer. So I decided to let Bel and Riot have a bit of a breather before whatever danger is in store for them in the next book. For this installment, I hope you simply enjoy their company.

for Jessie Vanek
every voracious reader deserves
at least one book dedication

"I do love nothing in the world so well as you: is not that strange?"
— Benedick in Much Ado About Nothing

DAY 99

THINGS BURIED

Thursday, June 21 1900

LILY WHITE SIPPED HER COFFEE, ENJOYING THE PEACE OF A CLEAN home, the scents of beeswax, polish, and a hint of lemon. The house was quiet, too. The boarders had come and gone like a train on schedule, steaming through the morning buffet with places to be.

Lily was exactly where she *wanted* to be, in a place that had become home. Home, a word she hadn't felt for quite some time. As she sat in silence with her coffee, she tallied up receipts, and made notations in the account books for Ravenwood Manor. When she reached the end of the pile, she stared at the final number.

Atticus Riot was near to broke. Not broke like most folk. He had this house, and plenty of assets to sell off, but he was broke by the standards of his class. Truth be told, she wasn't sure where he fit in with society, or even if he did at all.

It always happened to the good ones, she thought. That, and he had no mind for business. Thank the Lord, she did. But what could she do with so little savings left? Full partner as she now was, it took money to make money, and she was no miracle worker.

While Mr. Riot was a gambler, she was a business woman. Some said there was little difference. If that were true, then Lily was the cautious type. She preferred to have a sure bet before putting her money on the line.

She set down her pencil and frowned at the financials in the newspaper. Should she take the traditional route? Or—she glanced at a name and address she had written on a slip of paper —a less conventional path? Would Mr. Riot invest in the idea she had in mind? Well, as a full partner who had been given the reins, it was her decision. But was she biased—entertaining the idea of starting a business with a friend? New businesses were always a gamble.

Noise came from outside. Boots, running ones that could only belong to one person, her younger son. A knot unwound from between her shoulders and a buzz switched on in the back of her mind. Aah. Motherhood.

Lily sighed, and braced herself for what was to come. It was always something with Tobias White.

The door slammed open. A bit of plaster flaked off the abused wall. Tobias bolted straight for her and didn't slow until his arms were around her neck. As quickly as he came, he was gone, heading straight at the pie bin with a large grin.

"Tobias White, give a proper greeting to your mother and wash your hands."

"I'm too hungry for words."

The cuffs of his trousers showed more of his boots than she'd like. She swore he had grown another two inches in the four days he had been gone.

"Have you eaten breakfast?" she asked. Tobias was always starving. Two hours between meals and the boy was convinced he'd die.

"'Course not. There ain't no breakfast at sea."

"There *isn't any*," she corrected.

Tobias was drooling at the apple pie. Before he decided to help himself to a slice (and make a mess), she pushed back her chair and took up a knife. "Wash up first."

Tobias ran to the utility room sink. He ran *everywhere*. Lily didn't believe for one moment that her younger son had a source of boundless energy. She knew the truth. He sucked energy from everyone else around him and used it on the most useless things he could dream up. Tobias was back in a flash, leaving a trail of water dripping onto her freshly polished floors.

Lily handed her son a towel. He dried his hands, plopped on a chair, and took up his fork.

"Say your grace," Lily ordered.

"It's dessert," he argued.

"It's breakfast."

Tobias bowed his head and said a starving man's prayer. Lily let his brevity slide for the generous thanks he gave for his wonderful mother, and set the plate down. Half of the pie was gone in one gulp.

"How was your trip?" she asked.

Tobias's eyes widened as he chewed. Lily put away her ledgers and folded her papers. She sat, waiting, watching her son. Another bite replaced the first, but he'd run out of pie eventually. And she'd be waiting patiently.

The inevitable happened.

"That sure was good, Ma." Tobias hopped to his feet, wiping his hands on his coat.

"Did I excuse you, Tobias?"

Tobias sat back down with a "No, Ma'am. But I'm sworn to secrecy, you see. On pain of no sweets."

Despite herself, Lily snorted a laugh. She covered up her amusement by stirring some cream into her coffee. "Pain of no sweets? You can live with no sweets, child. You can't live without food, however."

"A shipmate don't rat out his captain."

"I think Mr. Tim is a bad influence on you."

Tobias's mouth fell open. That boy was about as subtle as a mime. "But it was Captain Morgan who ordered me to silence!" he said.

Lily blinked.

Tobias froze. His eyes got big as a cat's.

"Close your mouth when you eat," she ordered. "I'll pretend I didn't hear that."

Captain Morgan was a pseudonym for Isobel Amsel. Dear Lord. Isobel was supposed to be languishing in an asylum. Why on earth had she risked further punishment by leaving the asylum grounds?

Lily gave her son another piece of pie to silence him.

Another set of boots stomped at the back door. Mr. Tim shouldered it open and walked inside, carrying a dirt-encrusted box. He deposited his load on her table.

"Compliments of A.J.," Tim announced.

Lily glanced from the dingy box to the dingy man, who was patting his pockets and murmuring to himself.

Tobias reached into his coat pocket, swallowed, and held out a folded envelope." Mr. A.J. said you'd lose it."

Tim turned a furious blue eye on the boy. "I wasn't gonna lose it. A.J.'s just got a smart mouth on him. And no respect for his elders."

"You were there when he gave it to me."

Tim blew out a breath. "Ungrateful little—"

"Mr. Tim," Lily warned, holding out her hand.

"I was talkin' about A.J., not your son."

"Just so. Hand it over."

"Open it, Ma!" Tobias burst out.

"I was intending to." She set the envelope down. "Would you like coffee, Mr. Tim? Something to eat?"

"I can get it."

"Sit," she ordered. "I don't want you tracking any more mess in here."

Tim turned brick red. He cast his gaze over the floor, muttering to himself, and went off to wash up.

Tobias looked from his mother to the box. "Don't you want to know what's inside?"

"Is that box going anywhere?" Lily asked.

No answer.

With a nod, she lit the stove and went about cooking up an omelet and fresh coffee. Tobias sighed, raised his eyes to the ceiling, and melted halfway off the chair.

Drawn by the scent of food, Watson sauntered in from the hallway. Lily arched a brow at the plump cat, but he pointedly ignored her and began licking his claws.

"Will Mr. Riot and Sarah be here any time soon?" she asked when Tim returned. He scratched at his now damp beard.

"I'm not rightly sure. Jin is staying with Miss Bel at the asylum—"

"Where she belongs," Tobias muttered.

"And A.J. took Sarah off to wrap up a case. I wager he'll be back to Napa soon enough."

That was a great deal of traveling, but then love was an intoxicating thing. Lily placed coffee, eggs, and toast in front of the old man, who dug in with gratitude. His white beard made him look larger than he was, but Lily knew there wasn't much to the man. Bones lost their weight and muscles weakened as time wore on a body.

Tobias watched her through his lashes as she dried her hands and sat down. Just to annoy her son, she moved her coffee mug to the right, repositioned a vase, and began rearranging the flowers.

"Ma!"

Lily gave a slight smile as she sliced open the envelope. Mr. Riot had a steady, even hand, and he dotted his i's with precision. The envelope was addressed to her.

Miss Lily,

I can't do much to change the way of the world. But I can do this. It's not the mountain of gold you would prefer, but I believe a capable woman like yourself can turn it into one.

Bel is in agreement. My offer stands.

A mountain. Lily's conversation with Mr. Riot from a few days before came to mind, when he had asked her what she preferred.

"I'd prefer a qualified teacher who wasn't a prostitute. And I'd prefer not to have to worry about the color of my skin every time I leave this house."

"Anything else?" he had asked.

"I'd like the past to stay where it belongs, and I'd like my employer to stop using my young son as a spy." She had paused then. "A mountain of gold would be nice, too. What do you prefer?"

"To be at Bright Waters."

She grimaced at her words, at how close she had come to telling Mr. Riot everything. To a detective with ties to the Pinkertons, no less. As much as Ravenwood Manor felt like home, she was walking a dangerous line there.

Pushing the past back into a mental box, she turned to a physical one—the old rotting crate on her polished table. There was no lock, so she opened it. Red dirt, pebbles, and sand dribbled onto her table, but Lily didn't pay the filth any mind. She was transfixed. Gold. A box of gold Lady Liberty coins. Twenty dollars apiece.

Tim cackled at her shock.

Lily cleared her throat and picked up a coin. It was heavy. "Did Mr. Riot win this at a gambling table?" she demanded.

"It's buried treasure!" Tobias burst like a trumpet blast.

Tim shot the boy a glare. "Don't shout it to the rafters, boy. Good way to get it stolen."

Lily stared at Tim, waiting for an answer. Her son was prone to feats of imagination that would try a saint.

"It's as he says," Tim said between mouthfuls. "A finder's fee, you might say."

Lily opened the box, and did a quick estimate by the size of the box and the value of coins. There had to be close to twenty five hundred dollars in there.

"A.J. said you'd know what to do with that," Tim said.

"Where did you find it?" she asked.

Tobias didn't need further invitation. Her son launched into an all too brief summary about a case. "Some strange fellow was being followed. Turned out the stalker was his grandad's pirate buddy. They stole eggs. Then buried gold. I helped Mr. Riot find the map. It was on a box."

"Er, aye, that's the gist of it," Tim agreed.

Lily studied the gold coin in her hand. Why not, she thought? Pirates and buried treasure. Would her business proposal really be so strange?

DAY 90

LIES AND TRUTH

Saturday, June 30 1900

ISOBEL AMSEL STARED AT HER TWIN. DUMBFOUNDED WOULD BE the word—a state she was rarely in and would never admit to. But it would be difficult to deny it, with her mouth hanging slightly open like a fish. She clicked it shut.

"What do you mean you're *leaving*?"

"Shall I get a dictionary?" Lotario asked.

"I know what it means," she snapped. "*Why* are you leaving?"

Lotario waved a flippant hand. "I'm bored."

Isobel was, too. Only she couldn't leave. She sank into a chair and gazed numbly around her twin's rented cottage on Bright Waters's grounds. His trunks were thrown open and his clothes flung this way and that. For all his words, he didn't appear to be in a hurry. He sat there, sipping chilled tea and staring at his mess fully expecting his garments to sort themselves given enough time.

"You have a shadow to keep you occupied now," Lotario said into the silence.

Isobel glanced out the window to where Jin was climbing a tree. Since the girl had been introduced to the idea, her feet had hardly touched the ground. It was true though. Isobel did have a shadow. And to be honest, she enjoyed the diversion. Since Riot and Sarah had left, Isobel had taken to training Jin, devising elaborate exercises in tracking and lock picking. Not to mention schooling.

"I'm not worried about myself, Ari." Now that she'd had time to think it over, at any rate.

His brows shot up. "That's a first."

She considered throwing a shoe at him, but that would undermine her next words. "Your shoulder isn't healed yet."

Lotario raised said arm with only a minor wince, but his range of mobility was frightful. "I don't think the good doctor can do much more for me."

"What will you do?" she asked softly.

Her twin had numerous personas—identities that he actually *lived.* Not like her own blundering attempts at living other lives and lies. Lotario didn't live lies. Each persona was a piece of a puzzle that made a complete picture: Paris, a high-class burlesque dancer and male prostitute; Madame de Winter, an opera singer of some renown; and Lotario, flippant bachelor and traveler.

"Will you be able to dance with that shoulder as it is? What of your singing? How will you explain the scars on your shoulder?" Makeup would only hide so much.

"Don't worry, Bel," Lotario said with a roll of his eyes. She frowned, and he hesitated. When he spoke next, the whimsy was gone from his voice. "I mean that," he said.

"That is the opposite of reassuring."

"I'm not here to reassure you. You have three months left of your sentence. Jin is here. Atticus will return. I'm only in the way. Besides," he gestured at the cottage, "this place is paid for, through the day of your release. I've already checked with Julius. You can move from your single room into here."

Isobel stifled her surprise. Bright Waters's private cottages did not come cheap. Part pleasure retreat, part asylum, the hospital catered to both, and the cottages helped offset the cost of patients who couldn't afford its fees. Lotario's personas were profitable, and thus the cottage. Her persona had been, too. As the wife of Alex Kingston, she'd snagged a gold mine. Only Isobel had discovered that she could not live a lie.

When strong emotion threatened, Isobel put up her walls. She stood, intending to leave. "Will you go abroad?" she asked coolly.

But Lotario wouldn't let her withdraw. He wrapped his arms around her, and she let him, suffering through his display of emotion. But when he released her, it wasn't Lotario who had tears in his eyes.

Isobel scrubbed her palm against her cheeks.

"Tears, sister dear?"

"Allergies. Do be careful, Ari."

"Of course," he drawled, then frowned, eyes narrowing. "That won't work on me, you know."

"What?"

"Your tears."

"It's not a ploy," she insisted. "Do you really think me so cold-hearted?"

"I think you a horrid actor."

"You're disappearing with hardly a warning—"

"I'm telling you now."

"You're half healed from a bullet. Pale, exhausted, with no word of where you're heading. Of course I'm worried!" The last left her lips with more anger than intended.

Lotario sighed, and wiped a tear from her cheek. "I need to find myself again. I can't do that here," he whispered.

"Because there's no drinking and no endless parties to drown out the darkness?"

"A touch dramatic, don't you think?"

"No. It's the truth, and you know it."

"I *like* parties," he said with a click of teeth.

Silence.

Then Lotario sighed. "I don't want our final conversation to be in anger."

"I don't like the word 'final'."

"You really *are* worried."

Isobel clenched her jaw.

"Bel." He took her hands. "I don't have any extravagant plans to fake my own death the way you did."

Isobel took a breath.

"I'll see you again. I promise," he said.

Resigned, she accepted his words at face value. "Is there anything I can do for you?"

The corner of his lips curved like a cat. "There *is* something…" He gestured towards his trunks, and Isobel wondered if he too had been acting. She let herself be goaded into doing his bidding. It would give her a chance to pinch some of his clothes.

DAY 89

AVOIDANCE

Sunday, July 1 1900

Isobel knocked impatiently. Before anyone could hope to answer, she let herself into the room. Julius Bright looked up from his desk.

"Did you know Lotario left yesterday?" she demanded.

"Hello, Miss Amsel," Julius said in greeting. He gestured towards the door. "Generally people wait before coming in."

"Don't change the subject."

"Ignoring social cues is an indication of insanity."

"I'm already locked up," she said, closing the door.

"What if I'd had a patient?"

"Sunday is your day off. You don't see patients."

"And yet here I am working," he sighed. "And yes, I do have the occasional patient. Even on Sunday."

"You didn't this Sunday."

"And how could you possibly know that, Miss Amsel?"

"Julius," she warned. The good doctor likely suspected she had peeked at his appointment book. Which she had, but that was beside the point. "Lotario isn't recovered. He can barely use his arm."

Not a man to be rushed by the mentally disturbed, Julius calmly picked up a pen, and scratched her name into his appointment book. He capped the pen and sat back, waiting.

"I am *not* your appointment."

"You are now."

"Don't smile at me," she warned.

He smiled anyway. "Won't you sit?"

Isobel sat—on the edge of his desk.

Julius looked up at her. "I can't divulge information about a patient. And *do not* break into my files again, or I'll hand you over to Sheriff Nash," he said firmly.

"You're so paranoid," Isobel said.

"Are you going to sit there like a gargoyle arguing with me, or are you going to *talk* with me?"

Isobel plucked up his pen, fiddling with it. "I'm worried."

"Did you speak with Lotario before he left?"

"I did. That's why I'm worried." She began uncapping and recapping the pen. "He was vague and cryptic—"

"Both of you are generally vague and cryptic."

She ignored the observation. "Something is *wrong*."

"Aren't we all a little *wrong*?"

"According to you, I'm perfectly sane."

Julius smiled. "I said you *may* be the sanest person I've ever met. I haven't confirmed it yet."

"That doesn't speak highly of humanity."

"No, it doesn't," Julius said flatly. He leaned forward, all humor gone from his eyes. "As your friend, and not your doctor, I can assure you that this is the best thing for your twin. I've done all I can. The rest is up to him."

"He talked to you."

"That would be the obvious conclusion. But I can't confirm it."

"Right." Isobel stared at idyllic paintings of the countryside hanging on his office walls. "I'll miss him." She stood to leave.

"You mean you'll miss having him stand in for your talking sessions."

She arched a brow. "How long have you known?"

"I first suspected when you 'slipped' while getting out of a bathtub and injured the same shoulder as your brother."

"I only have two shoulders. The chance of injuring the same one as Ari is rather high."

Julius huffed.

"Why didn't you say something?" she asked.

"I found it most diverting. And from a clinical standpoint, fascinating. If it makes you feel any better, I'm not entirely sure who was who on every occasion."

"We know," she said. "It's part of the ruse. Ari and I did it to our mother all the time. It kept her guessing."

"Ah." He sat back, stunned. "So sometimes you act as your brother playing yourself? And vise versa?"

Isobel nodded.

"Disguise within disguise. I don't suppose you'd write down who was present at each session?"

Isobel straightened a painting of a horse. The muted colors and bland trees made her want to rip it off the wall. "I could," she said over her shoulder. "But you're too much of a friend, so I'll tell you now that it'd all be lies."

Julius chuckled. "I appreciate it. Life's mysteries, I suppose, keep us going."

Isobel turned. "*Solving* them keeps us going, Doctor."

"I doubt I'll ever solve this one," he said, resigned. "Lotario has offered you his cottage. You don't need to remain in the ward room." He held out a hand. Isobel stared at it, then realized she had tucked his pen away. She handed it over.

"Won't you get in trouble with the authorities?" she asked.

"I'll call it 'solitary confinement'."

Isobel snorted. "So now I can suffer tedium in a holiday cottage."

"Tedium or avoidance," he mused.

"I beg your pardon?"

"Avoidance. Have you considered that you're running away from yourself?"

"I'm not here for a talking session."

"You barged into *my* office."

"Out of concern for Lotario."

"Well you're still here."

She turned to leave.

"*Isobel.*"

She stopped at the use of her given name.

"You can't relax. I understand that. But you have a family now. For the sake of those you love, find a way to *be* with *yourself.*"

Her hand was stuck on the knob. She felt frozen, unable to leave or stay, caught in the between. "I'm not here of my own free will, Doctor," she said softly.

"No. You're here because a powerful man threatened your family, blackmailed you, and cornered you into marriage and his bed. Then your older brother tried to murder you." Each word hit her in the back. "Some would feel blessed to recuperate here, and they'd gladly switch places with you. Don't waste what time you have left. *Accept* my help."

Isobel let out a shaky breath. "Only if we talk as friends."

"I believe we have been for some time."

"And not here." She gestured sharply at the paintings. "I'm half-tempted to burn them."

Julius pushed back his chair, and grabbed his coat. "Most find them soothing."

"Art is subjective."

"Hmm."

They walked out of the ward into fresh air. She breathed in the heat of the day, and turned her face towards the sun. "Can we walk to town?"

"Why?" he asked suspiciously.

"I need to send a telegram."

"To whom?"

"Are you my child-minder?" she snapped.

"No, I'm the alienist tasked with trying to 'rehabilitate' you, and sorely regretting it."

Isobel started to dig in for the sake of it, but relented. "I want to send a telegram to Riot. Since you're bound by whatever code alienists follow, I'll simply ask Riot to check on Ari. Is that allowed?"

"I'll keep you to your word about talking with me."

"My dear doctor, you should have specified what we were going to talk about."

"Isobel," he warned.

They walked for a time, enjoying the song of birds and rustle of leaves. Isobel always felt better when she stretched her legs. But she could feel the doctor's growing discontent. He likely worried the entire conversation had been a ploy to get him to escort her into town.

"I chose my course," she said suddenly. "Alex didn't force me. He outmaneuvered me. I simply couldn't keep up the ruse."

"So say any number of prostitutes."

Isobel glanced up at the tall man. "Are you calling me a whore?"

"Do you consider that an insult?" he countered.

"Society does."

"And yet few men have qualms about buying their services."

"Do you?" she asked, curious.

Julius blushed. "I… erm… don't generally discuss such matters with friends."

"But you're an alienist. Surely you're comfortable discussing sexual matters. Your colleagues certainly find human sexuality a fascinating subject. Or is it because I'm a woman?"

Julius adjusted his tie. "It's not that," he said. "It's… for the same reason Lotario doesn't discuss it."

Isobel blinked, and after a bloated moment, realization set in. "Oh. I had no idea."

"I'm relieved."

Isobel smiled.

"Regardless, I find the required mindset of the profession unhealthy. There are perhaps a few women, and men, who enjoy that work. But the vast majority are bullied, coerced, or forced into the profession by circumstance." He stopped and stared down at her. "And to survive in that profession one must convince oneself that it was, and *is*, one's choice."

Isobel took in his words. They were heavy with implication.

"You think I'm lying to myself," she said.

"Aren't you?"

"Don't we all lie to ourselves to survive?" she countered.

"To an extent, but is that healthy?"

They turned and began walking again. "It's a means to an end."

"And what is your end, Isobel?"

"I'm no fortune teller."

"Neither am I, but I do see a pattern in you and your twin. You are both self-destructive."

"I call it living life."

"Just so. I asked Lotario why he lives that way. And I think he went off to find the answer."

"Or he got bored."

"That, too," Julius admitted.

Still, Isobel considered his words. She wasn't one to shy away from uncomfortable truths waved in her face.

"Perhaps my twin and I don't feel worthy of love because we ruined our mother's health when we were born. Our births nearly killed her, you know? She's used a cane ever since. So we behave in a manner to discourage love."

Julius clasped his hands behind his back, nodding. And then he stopped, glancing down at her with suspicion. "You don't sound convinced."

"It's a good answer though, isn't it? Suitable for an alienist's diagnosis. You can write it down in our files," she said, pleased with herself.

Julius grunted. "Do you have another theory? One that isn't suitable for my clinical notes?"

"I do, actually," she said. "We aren't self-destructive. Our minds rail against convention. We rebel for the sake of it."

"And yet you're getting married and adopting two children. That sounds mundane to me."

"I'm marrying a man with the surname of *Riot*. Does that strike you as conventional?"

"And if your marriage proves conventional?"

Isobel's only answer was a sharp laugh.

DAY 88

A CHILD'S WISDOM

Monday, July 2 1900

Atticus Riot stared at a display of rings, all encrusted with diamonds, sapphires, and rubies like barnacles on a golden hull nestled in a velvet sea.

"That one is nice." Sarah pointed to a ring set with a large sapphire surrounded by diamonds. The jeweler beamed at Riot's adoptive daughter.

"It's a *Cartier* design—a jeweler to royalty." The jeweler glanced at Riot, over to Sarah, then removed the ring, slipping it on the girl's finger.

Sarah gaped at the brilliance. "I think Isobel would *love* this." Sarah had said that about every ring in the last three shops. Although she did sound adamant about this one. Riot checked the price. Sarah had expensive taste.

"Did you have something specific in mind, sir?" asked the wizened jeweler.

"No, but I'll know when I see it," Riot said.

"We do craft custom rings, sir. We could sit down and discuss the preferences of the lady in question. It's my business to help gentlemen like yourself find the perfect ring for his future wife."

Riot rubbed his beard in consideration. "Not today, but thank you all the same."

With reluctance, Sarah returned the ring, and followed Riot outside into the bustle of Market Street. Riot took a deep breath, gripping his walking stick until his knuckles turned white. Sarah slipped her arm through his, and sighed. "The ring was gorgeous, don't you think?" Her freckled face had a dreamy look to it.

"It was a fine ring," he agreed.

"You said that about every ring we looked at that I liked."

"They weren't…" Riot cocked his head, searching for the word. "Right for Bel."

"What *is* right for Isobel?"

Such a simple question. And straight to the point.

Riot looked down into wide, innocent eyes, and he found he didn't have an answer. Only a vague uneasiness. "Lunch?" he asked instead.

"We haven't found a ring yet," Sarah countered.

Riot inclined his head towards the Palace Hotel, and the girl's eyes brightened. Sarah would never turn down lunch at the Palace. She gave in to his offer with a determined "But we're going back to find a ring afterwards."

The maitre d' greeted Riot with a smile.

"We'll take that table by the wall over there," Riot said before the man could choose one.

"But, sir, that isn't—"

"I'd like to sit there all the same." Riot slipped him a tip.

"Of course."

They threaded their way through elegance, a bloom of light, palm fronds, and clinking cutlery—all the way to the back of the dining room, near the kitchen.

Riot held a chair out for Sarah, then settled himself opposite with his back to the wall. At a sweep of his gaze, a few diners noticed him, hastily paid their bills and headed for the door, the sting of guilt between their shoulders.

Riot focused on his menu, and felt the touch of eyes. Sarah was squinting at him.

"Do you need spectacles?" he asked.

Sarah started. "What?"

"Spectacles." He adjusted his own.

Sarah blushed and quickly hid behind her menu. A sharp waiter appeared. "May I get you something to drink while you peruse our menu?"

Riot ordered Young Hyson tea, and French bread and butter for the table. The waiter left, stepping through a swinging door. Their table's proximity to the kitchen made it a noisy spot. The only benefit was the quickness with which the waiter returned. By that time Riot and Sarah were ready with the rest of their order.

When the waiter had left, Riot sat back and stared at his daughter. "What's on your mind, Sarah?"

Sarah poked at a piece of bread with her butter knife. "I would have worn a nicer dress if I knew we were coming here," she said quietly.

"You look lovely, Sarah."

But his words only made her shift in her chair. She glanced at a pair of women, dressed in resplendent finery, sitting in a pool of light in the center of the room. In a flash, Riot caught the shame in Sarah's eyes, put it together with his request for a seat in the back of the room, and understood. Who knew parenthood required so much deduction?

"I didn't request this table because I was ashamed of you."

She looked up, surprised. "Then why'd we sit all the way back here?" The door to the kitchen swung open. A glass shattered from inside, and what sounded like a tumbling tray. An abrupt curse cut off as the door swung closed. It was not the best of tables—not from a diner's point of view, but then Riot wasn't simply a diner. He was a detective with a price on his head. And far too many enemies.

He made an unconscious sweep of the room, noting those he recognized—potential threats and old allies—and suspicious bulges and handbags large enough to conceal a revolver. The exits. Cover. Trays that might stop a bullet, and the quickest way to get Sarah to safety. All in a flash of thought that came from a lifetime of threat.

Riot smiled easily. "Old habits."

Sarah frowned at him. She wasn't about to buy his explanation. She was far too wise, and he loved the girl for it.

"I feel better with my back to a wall, an exit readily at hand, and a view of the entrance."

Understanding lit Sarah's eyes a few moments later. She started, hunched down, and glanced over her shoulder. "You're worried someone is going to start shooting at us."

Riot inclined his head. "I didn't make it to the ripe old age of forty by being careless."

Sarah leaned towards him and whispered, "Who's the person?"

Riot patted her hand. "No one in particular. I'm a careful man, Sarah. That's all. Especially where you are concerned."

"Shouldn't I be sitting with my back to a wall, too?"

"If you like, but it's only a precaution. Try not to be obvious though."

She scooted her chair around, so she had a better view of the dining room. "So what are you looking for?"

Riot buttered a piece of bread, and covertly eyed the room. "Anything that pricks my instincts."

She sighed. "That's not helpful."

"Isn't it?"

Sarah ate her bread, considering. Finally, she glanced at him.

"Wouldn't it be easier just to poison the butter?" She nodded towards his bread. "If someone wanted to kill you?"

Riot stopped chewing for a moment. He swallowed. "Fortunately, most guns for hire aren't that imaginative."

"I suppose it'd take some planning, too."

Riot nodded. "More so than a quick draw and a bullet."

"If you're so brilliant and dangerous, how come you can't pick a ring?" Sarah asked.

Riot dabbed at his lips with a napkin. "I've never picked out a ring for a lady before. I'm treading in unfamiliar territory."

"I've never done most things before. You'll never do it till you do it," she said.

"What do you advise in this circumstance?"

Sarah thought. Not a show of it, but actual consideration. Sarah knew he wasn't just humoring her. Her opinion mattered to him.

"I don't think I've ever seen Isobel wear jewelry, unless she's in some sort of disguise. Will she even *care* what sort of ring she has?

"I doubt it."

"Then just get her any old ring."

Riot studied the tea leaves in his cup. It was a good suggestion, so why the hesitation? Why the doubt? Was marriage even right for a woman like Isobel? Would she find it too restricting, too suffocating after a mere month? Had he rushed things?

No, he thought. Isobel was not a woman to be rushed. She knew her mind. So was *he* having cold feet? The mere thought of spending the rest of his life without her seized his heart. And there it was. That passion terrified him.

Riot had spent his youth untamed—a quick hand with a quicker trigger. Ravenwood had taught him to bridle his emotions, to keep himself on a tight leash, because they both knew what Riot was capable of when he broke free of that leash. But Isobel… Isobel knew that, too. As no one else did.

Their food came: *Aiguillette of Flounder* and *Creole potatoes persillade* for Riot, and a broiled pork cutlet and apple sauce for Sarah.

Riot picked up his fork and knife and slipped a bite of flounder into his mouth. Delicately cooked, and savory. He made an appreciative sound, and stopped chewing when he saw Sarah's shock.

"You didn't say grace."

Riot swallowed. "I generally don't."

"I noticed."

"I haven't been saying grace for quite awhile."

"You weren't my father before," Sarah pointed out. "And this is a proper meal."

"Would you care to?"

"I think you're supposed to."

Riot set down his cutlery, and cleared his throat. "Grace."

Sarah snorted, then with a roll of eyes, clasped her hands and bowed her head. "Lord, thank you for this meal, and don't mind my father, he has a good heart. Amen."

The girl began eating, oblivious to his silence.

After a time, she noticed. "Did I offend you?"

Riot shook his head. "I'm more likely to be the one to offend you."

"It's all right," Sarah said. "Can't force someone one way, but my gramma sure tried."

"She must have been a remarkable woman."

Sarah wrinkled her nose. "Even the preacher steered clear of her."

Riot's lip quirked.

"I suppose she was a lot like Isobel's mother," Sarah mused. "Without the cane. But she was warm, and, oh, was she kind. She'd take in vagabonds. Well… let them sleep in our barn 'cause it wasn't proper otherwise. And she'd always knit socks and caps, and make quilts, and share our food with larger families. But here's the nicest thing about her… she'd always accept payment of some sort. To save their pride. People don't like charity. She was always careful about that."

"You have her kindness," Riot said.

Sarah blushed. "Thank you. What about your parents?"

Riot grimaced at the innocent question. "I don't know. I'm an orphan like yourself."

"I don't know if it counts being an orphan since my gramma was there to take care of me. You don't remember anything?" she asked with a hint of sorrow.

Riot remembered the slow creak of a straining rope, and toes. Dirty toes hanging above the floor. He shoved the memory aside, and focused on something else. "My mother had a soft voice. And she told me stories." The last was a lie. But then a very young Riot had told himself those lies to survive.

"About what?"

"Of little boys who grew up to be knights. And talking toads. And kingdoms of ants."

Sarah smiled, a bright one that chased back the creeping darkness in his heart. "My gramma didn't have any kind of imagination."

"It is a gift," Riot agreed.

Sarah's eyes widened. "Say! That's where you get a ring. From family. Did your mother have a ring?"

"I'm afraid not." Riot's mother had been picked clean by thieves while he screamed for them to cut her down. "She was poor, and unmarried."

"Oh." Sarah didn't ask any more questions, thankfully. "I forgot."

Riot hadn't told her about his stained lineage, but the girl read newspapers, and the papers had sung about his whoring mother clear across the United States.

"My gramma left me her ring. You can have it for Isobel."

"That's very generous of you, Sarah, but that's yours to wear. Don't part with a treasure like that."

Sarah poked at her food. "That's it… isn't it? You don't have a family ring to give Isobel?"

The question took him by surprise. A rare thing for someone like him. Had a freckled-faced twelve-year-old just flayed his emotions bare? She had.

Riot cocked his head, amused. "Maybe so." The answer was a relief.

"Well you best figure out what to do. You only have three months."

DAY 84

ANOTHER BROTHER

Friday, July 6 1900

Atticus Riot navigated a maze of salvage and new construction. The Saavedra Shipyards hummed with activity. It appeared organized and tightly run, and to have fully recovered from Alex Kingston's attempted sabotage.

Boats hugged the cove, sitting on high timbers, their hulls resting in cradles over muddy beaches. A few pleasure yachts dotted the shipyard, but it was mostly full of trawlers.

"Whatcha 'ere fir, sir?" a shirtless man hollered from atop a hull growing barnacles. It wasn't high up, but with the saws, hammering, shouts, and seagulls, it required a voice that carried.

"I was told a cutter by the name of the *Pagan Lady* was brought here for salvage."

"The who?"

Riot raised his voice. "The *Pagan Lady*!"

"The foreman's that way." The man pointed. Apparently working conditions made the ears go prematurely.

Riot searched the yard for the foreman or the *Lady*. The yellow slip of paper in his breast pocket lightened his step. One cryptic request from Isobel, and he had dropped everything to appease her. It was a new sensation. 'My reflection left', the telegram read. 'I don't know why.'

Surprisingly, the fervor from Isobel's trial had not diminished. Reports about Isobel's most recent case had been blasted all over the newspapers. Not the truth. Never that. But news that she had been key in the rescue of two missing boys had generated yet another reporting frenzy. Those same reporters liked to lurk around telegraph offices intercepting messages. For that reason, their telegram exchanges had to be cryptic.

Cryptic for others. But not Riot. She was worried about Lotario. He could feel her frustration in that brief request. Trapped. Unable to leave while the world spun on its merry way.

Riot rounded a hull and was confronted by a large man wielding an adze. Muscles rippled with each powerful swing, and workers gathered to watch his skill. He was hollowing one half of a mast. The other half, which would be fitted with its twin, had already been completed.

When the man was satisfied, he handed the adze to another. He was over six feet tall with white blond hair and a bushy beard. His shoulders rippled with tanned muscle, while his stomach made it clear he was a man who liked his beer. He was a beefier version of his father—Marcus Amsel. But not his eyes. Emmett Amsel had gotten his piercing gray eyes from his mother and the Germanic bearing of a Saxon from his father. It wasn't difficult to picture this man charging the walls of Rome.

Emmett glanced at Riot, who stood nearby, waiting. Riot had met Isobel's older brother once before. At Isobel's funeral.

"Mr. Riot." Emmett's words were neither welcoming nor hostile. The large man turned back to his workers. "Put the battens in, tie them together, and paint the ends."

Emmett grabbed a towel, and wiped his chest. "Have you come to shoot me, Mr. Riot?" Emmett was about Riot's own age.

Perhaps five years younger than the elder brother, Curtis, whom Riot had reportedly killed. Had the brothers been close?

"I wasn't planning on it," Riot said easily. "Business appears to be booming again." It was a subtle reminder of the events surrounding Curtis's death. And the mess the elder brother had dragged the family into.

Emmett grunted. "It is." The larger man struck off without a word, forcing Riot to follow. "Are you still planning on marrying my little sister?" Emmett asked.

"If she'll have me."

Emmett stopped, and turned to face him. Riot had to tilt his hat back to meet the man's sharp eyes. Emmett gripped Riot's shoulder and squeezed. His grip was staggering.

"You know, little man, we have a tradition in our family." Emmett jerked Riot close. "We lash suitors to a mast in a storm, and let the sea decide if they're worthy."

"How did your wife fare during that trial?" Riot asked.

Emmett's lips tightened, and he narrowed his eyes. Riot felt like he was looking into the eye of a storm. And then the visage cracked. Emmett boomed a laugh, and slapped Riot so hard on the back that he took a step forward to catch himself.

"You're lucky my mother likes you." Another slap on the back drove the air from Riot's lungs. The big man slapped him again to get him breathing, and Riot gulped in a lungful of air.

"I'm more concerned with Isobel's opinion," Riot said with a cough.

"Phah! Isobel is worse than the wind." Emmett marched over to a shack, and grabbed a shirt from inside. He shrugged it on, but it did little to conceal his broad chest. A button had already popped in the center. "Business *is* good," he admitted, a shadow of grief and guilt flickering across his eyes. "It's unfortunate it was ever bad."

Riot didn't reply. There were no words to soothe family betrayal.

"Why have you come?" Emmett asked.

"I heard the *Pagan Lady* was brought here."

Emmett grumbled. "It's called the *Osprey*."

"Why did you have it moved?" On paper, Riot owned the *Pagan Lady*. He had purchased it in his name for Isobel, and hired 'Captain Morgan' to pilot it.

"I didn't have it moved. My brother did."

"Lotario?" Riot asked.

Emmett nodded, stroking his beard. "I was surprised to see him… and that boat. It gives me some hope that he might stay and work."

"You'd like that?" Riot asked, surprised.

Emmett rumbled. "Lotario is an artist. He doesn't look like much, but he has a way with boats. Even better than Vicilia. Lotario worked with us when he was younger."

"I thought he worked with your father?"

"My father is a passable boatbuilder, but he's a better winemaker. Lotario was the one who built that boat. Father helped *him*." It was the most Riot had ever heard out of the big man. But then he barely knew him. And that appeared to be all Emmett was willing to say. Emmett pointed Riot to a large workshop. "She's in there."

The *Lady* rested on a cradle of timbers. She looked embarrassed. Stripped bare, her accoutrements neatly laid to one side, a perfume of pine and oakum permeated the air. A gaping wound in her side showed her ribs.

Riot suppressed a shudder. The dark. The cold. A sinking death trap, and a single hatch blocking his path to air. He had always wagered he'd die by a bullet. Not water. Somehow the first seemed preferable.

Noise came from within the hull, and a familiar face poked

through. "Contemplating mortality, Atticus?" Lotario Amsel drawled. His hair was shaggy, and the dye was fast fading. Exactly like Isobel's. Had the two of them sat down and discussed whether or not they'd grow their hair out? Or was it instinctual?

"I was, actually," Riot said.

"Dark, handsome, *and* brooding. My lucky day. Have you come to inspire me, or did you need something?"

"I came to check on the *Lady*."

"Which one?" Lotario asked.

"Isobel is worried about you."

"Why else would her knight errant come to spy on me?"

"Spies don't usually announce their intent," Riot said.

"Well, you're an honorable sort. I hope you weren't searching for me overly long."

The edge of Riot's lip quirked. "I've had plenty of practice." He nodded towards the hull. "Why strip her down? Can't you just patch her?"

"I *could*," Lotario drawled from inside. "But where's the fun in that? Besides, I have some ideas, and I intend to reinforce her so she'll be fit to smash ice."

"We were planning on having the *Lady* repaired. You don't have to do all of this."

"Who says I'm doing it for you?" came the muffled reply. Wood screeched as Lotario tugged free another plank. "I sold you my pride and joy, and look what you did to her. I may just take her back."

Riot climbed a short ladder, and peered through the gaping hole. The deck was missing, the insides gutted. Riot wasn't a sentimental man, but something caught in his throat. Isobel loved this boat, and her life currently mirrored its state. It was a shambles.

A hand touched his shoulder. "She'll be fine," Lotario said softly, and then turned away from the breach.

Riot wasn't sure if he meant the boat or Isobel, but he got his first good look at Lotario. Lotario wore a loose shirt, open at the front, cuffs rolled up to his forearms. He looked like a French painter straight from the Renaissance era. There was a tool belt on his hips, and a pencil tucked behind an ear. Rulers, hammers, chisels, and squares were laid out nearby. Along with a roll of paper that Lotario paused to consult.

"This appears to be a large undertaking. Do you have help?" Riot asked, noting the way Lotario held his left hand close to his stomach.

Lotario didn't look up from the plans. "I have you."

"I'm afraid I'm not much of a boatbuilder, or a builder of anything for that matter."

Lotario looked over his shoulder, arching a brow. "Atticus Riot can't swing a hammer?"

Riot *had* swung hammers before. Just never in the act of creating. It was more destructive, or as an improvised weapon whenever he was in a bind.

"Don't worry," Lotario drawled.

"I'm not worried, I'm only warning you."

Lotario ignored Riot's assertion. "I won't tell a soul," he crooned. "On one condition."

"That being?" Riot asked, playing along.

"That you don't tell Bel what I'm about."

"Why can't she know?" Riot asked.

"It's a secret. It won't be much of one if I tell you."

"What *can* I tell her, then?"

"That I'm in good spirits, and my shoulder is fine." It was clearly not fine, his left hand was trembling. Riot gave the injured limb a pointed look.

Lotario made an exasperated sound. "*Fine.* You wrenched it out of me with your silence. Truth be told, I was tired of the exercises," Lotario admitted. "I thought maybe…" He placed his left hand on the hull. "We could heal together."

Riot nodded. Hard work, he had heard, could be therapeutic. As long as it wasn't detective work, at any rate. Riot set aside his hat and stick, and shrugged out of his coat. "What can I do?"

"You can keep stripping," Lotario said, openly watching. "You should really charge for the show, though."

"I'll keep that in mind when I'm broke," Riot said as he rolled up his sleeves.

"I'm serious. I'd take my shirt off if I were you," Lotario said.

Riot crossed his arms, and Lotario huffed, "I'm not being brazen. That's an expensive shirt, and I don't want you ruining it." He handed Riot a large scraper. "You do know how to scrape a hull, don't you?"

That was one thing Riot *did* know how to do. And cook.

Scraping barnacles off a hull was rough work. It was hot, too, and Miss Lily had just washed and starched his shirt. Lotario had a point. Riot removed his holster, unbuttoned his waistcoat, shirt, and undershirt, and set them aside.

Thankfully, Lotario kept his comments to himself.

Riot threw himself into the task. It felt good—simple, honest work without puzzles or complications. Without death or threat, and without a life on his shoulders. He worked until a sheen of sweat covered him, and his shoulders and back ached with the exertion.

Having long since removed his spectacles, Riot was surprised when a canteen was thrust in his face. He stopped, and gladly drank the offered water.

"You *have* done this before," Lotario said.

Riot grunted, handing the canteen back to the man. Lotario's eyes flickered to Riot's chest, and quickly looked away, taking a long gulp. His eyes drifted back to Riot's flesh—to the scars that screamed of a dangerous life.

"How…" Lotario hesitated, screwing the cap back on. "How did you heal?" he asked softly. Color rose to Lotario's cheeks, something Riot had never seen before. The man was blushing. "You make my *one* bullet scar look like a paper cut."

No innuendo. No light quip.

"I'm not sure I'm fully healed. But Isobel helped me take that first step," Riot said.

Lotario nodded. "She *is* special. We're lucky to have her."

They were, Riot thought. And she was special. Isobel deserved so much more than anything Riot could ever give her.

Lotario started to climb back up the ladder into the hull, but Riot placed a gentle hand on his bad shoulder, stopping him short.

"Your scars are a badge of honor for saving Bel's life," Riot said. "My scars are regret and vengeance. You'll heal with time."

Lotario arched a brow. Riot dropped his hand, but Lotario grabbed it and held on tightly. "I'm not the only one who saved a life that day. Regret, vengeance, whatever those scars of yours are, they put you in that courthouse. I certainly can't loathe them as you do." Lotario let go of his hand. "I know Bel doesn't. And neither should you."

DAY 74

B-E-A-R

Sunday, July 15 1900

JIN SCRATCHED OUT A SENTENCE, AND SHOVED THE PAPER ACROSS the table. Isobel looked up from her stack of books. She was determined to give the child a well-rounded education, ranging from mathematics, to poisons, to anatomy—subjects a ten-year-old would be sure to enjoy. Isobel had always found school boring. Like herself, Jin had too inquisitive a mind to waste on the mundane. Isobel would turn the girl into a genius in no time.

Julius thought Isobel ought to find another hobby.

Isobel added a book of American law onto her growing stack, and glanced at Jin's latest efforts. She suppressed a sigh. "You put b-a-r-e. It's b-e-a-r."

"It is the same word," Jin said.

"It is spelled differently."

"But it *sounds* the same when spoken. Why does it matter?" Jin demanded.

"B-a-r-e means naked. The way you have it written, it reads, 'There was a naked in the woods'."

"I assumed you were not stupid, and would know what I meant," Jin shot back. "Like 'read' and 'read'. Why is one not r-e-d?"

"Because 'red' is a color."

"Then why isn't it r-e-e-d?"

"That's a plant."

Jin slammed her fists on the table. "They are all the same sounds when read aloud. You know what I mean in that sentence."

"Context."

"Exactly!" Jin snatched up her papers and crumpled them into tight little 'fury' balls before tossing them onto the ground.

Isobel swallowed down her frustration. Jin wasn't dumb. She was only logical. And English was not logical in the least. "You are correct," Isobel said with a calmness which would have impressed Riot. "If someone writes 'I red a book'. A discerning person will know what the writer is trying to say given the context of the sentence. But the reader will also come to the conclusion that the writer is uneducated. Do you want to appear uneducated?"

"I *am* uneducated."

"I'm trying to rectify that."

"You are doing a horrible job!" Jin fumed. A moment passed, then she balled her hands into fists, and looked down at them. "I'm sorry," came a whispered apology.

"Jin, I know you have an excellent memory. Remembering bare versus bear won't tax you. So what is the issue?"

"It's stupid! You tell me there are rules. But then some words ignore the rules. There is always a 'but'."

"I'll tell you one hard and fast rule." Isobel held up a finger. "Poor grammar makes a certain kind of person believe you are an idiot."

"I'm not an idiot."

"No, nor are those who can't read or write, or speak another language. Poor grammar can be used to mislead. And so can proper pronunciation and grammar."

This got Jin's attention.

"You can become someone else, shock, disarm, make people underestimate you, or even intimidate. Words can be wielded like a weapon. There's a saying: 'The pen is mightier than the sword.'"

"I would rather have a sword."

"Both are useful," Isobel agreed.

Jin sighed. "I have never even seen a bear. My *Bahba* never got to take me to the circus."

There was a longing there. An overwhelming wave of sadness that threatened to drown the child. Isobel frowned at her books. Decided, she hopped to her feet and snatched a satchel off its hook. She started tossing supplies inside.

"What are you doing?" Jin asked.

"It's too gorgeous to spend inside. Let's practice our tracking."

"It's hot out there."

"Yes, exactly. Sun is good for the mind."

"What are we tracking?" Jin asked.

"Let's go find a bear."

"A bear?"

"Yes, the furry kind. Not the naked."

"I do not think that is a good idea."

Isobel waggled a pen at the girl. "We'll have a sword with us."

"But—"

"Enough letters, and no buts," Isobel said, tugging off her dress. She reached for shirt and trousers.

"I will try harder." Jin stood stiffly in the middle of the cottage. "You do not need to leave me with a bear. I promise."

Isobel paused at the buttons on her shirt and squinted at the girl. "I'm not going to *feed* you to a bear, Jin."

"Will you leave me out there? In the wilderness?"

Isobel thrust a pair of small boots at the child. “I wouldn’t inflict that kind of torture on a poor bear.”

DAY 70

INTERLUDE

Friday, July 20 1900

"I FOUND ITS FOOTPRINTS BY A STREAM, AND TRACED IT ALL THE way back to the rocks." Jin pointed towards the Palisades. "But Isobel would not let me go into the cave." Jin's disappointment did little to diminish her animated story. The girl was as excited as Isobel had ever seen her.

Riot and Sarah had arrived at noon, and now Isobel walked beside Riot in Bright Waters' gardens, fully aware of the man. He listened to Jin with quiet interest. His trim beard carried faint scents of sandalwood and myrrh, and Isobel basked in his presence. Every nerve-ending in her body seemed attached to him.

His fingertips brushed the ends of hers, and it felt like a current of electricity passed between them. Isobel swallowed. Was he as aware of her? Would she ever be able to think straight when he was near?

Isobel didn't dare make eye contact with him. She didn't know if she could restrain herself.

"So we left an apple there, and another, and another," Jin continued. "A trail of apples right down to a meadow."

"Bears love apples," Sarah nodded sagely.

"I found a spot downwind and we waited, watching the pile of apples."

"Least you didn't cover yourself with honey. Some neighbor boys did that once—"

"*I* am telling the story, Sarah," Jin bit out.

Sarah muttered an apology. And Jin took a breath. "I would like to hear your story afterwards."

That was progress, Isobel thought.

"The bear," Riot prodded.

Jin walked on the other side of Riot, her face turned towards him, eyes alight. "It came out of the cave, and it stopped to eat each apple. It was bigger than you! And when it reached the pile, it sat on its rump, and began eating like a person. We stayed very still. I think it's like a dog-cat," she added. "And afterwards, it fell over. I thought Isobel poisoned the apples."

Isobel looked sharply at the girl.

"I said I *thought*. But the bear was only stuffed, and it slept in the sun. We snuck away while it was napping. And it is spelled b-e-a-r," Jin said matter-of-factly.

Sarah gave her sister a puzzled look.

"We have been studying English every day," Jin explained.

"I hope you can *bear* the workload," Riot said.

Jin narrowed her eyes, while Sarah rolled hers.

"Did you just make a *pun*, Riot?" Isobel asked, appalled.

"I would never do such a thing," he said, dryly.

"Is it b-e-a-r or b-a-r-e? Or is it b-e-e-r?" Jin asked.

"It's b-e-a-r," Sarah said.

Jin stomped her foot and growled. "How many other words make no sense!"

"Remind me to explain British vocabulary sometime," Riot said.

Jin waited. "Now?"

"No, not now." Isobel made a shooing motion at the girls. "Go get into trouble. The non-lethal kind."

Both girls looked at her in confusion.

"Wouldn't you rather be away from your parents?"

Jin smirked, and tugged on Sarah's sleeve. "Come on. They are going to kiss. It will be disgusting."

Sarah turned bright red. And the two ran down the pathway out of sight. Isobel waited to make sure the girls weren't hiding behind a bush. When she was satisfied, she turned to Riot. And she did kiss him—a flick of her tongue, and a small taste was all she allowed herself.

Isobel pulled back, staying in the circle of his arms. "I'll have to speak to Jin about appropriate conversation topics again."

"I'm not sure we're shining models of propriety. Besides, she was right." Riot pulled Isobel closer, his hand trailing down her back, his lips exploring hers until she melted against him with a moan. Isobel forgot where she was, and quite possibly who. She was dimly aware of his hat falling to the ground, and a breathless whisper that couldn't possibly be her voice.

"We can barricade ourselves in the cottage."

They nearly forgot his hat.

SOMETIME LATER, RIOT LAY IN A TANGLE OF LIMBS AND BEDDING, his clothing strewn about the bedroom. Isobel was sprawled on top of him. Propriety be damned, they'd broken all the rules. In the middle of the day, no less.

Riot smiled. A rare, unguarded one. He couldn't help it.

Isobel toyed with the hair on his chest, running her palm over muscle, bone, and scars. Sun shone through the open window, and he marveled at her hair—the red gold threads breaking through the fading dye. He cradled her close, and put his nose in her hair, inhaling her scent. Skin damp from perspiration, she smelled like the sun and trees, of something wild. He was drunk on her—the way she fit against his body, the way he fit inside of hers.

"What is it?" she asked.

"Impropriety has never felt so right."

Isobel laughed. "Would it feel half as good if we did things properly?"

Riot touched her cheek, drawing her eyes to his. "Yes. It still will," he whispered.

"You sound sure of that, Riot."

"It will involve you. That's sure enough for me."

"And when the attraction fades?" She wasn't being flippant. Only logical. Assessing all possibilities, all outcomes, and exploring the intricacies of emotion with unflinching honesty.

"Will it?" he asked in return.

Gray eyes sharpened. "I don't know."

"I'm willing to volunteer for your study. For the sake of research."

"You're mocking me."

"Considering where your knee is resting, I would never dream of it."

Isobel snorted, and pressed herself closer. "I have a vested interest in keeping you healthy and whole, my love."

The words came so easily, so thoughtlessly that it surprised Isobel. She paused, and then stretched to kiss his lips. A tender touch.

"I think that answers that," he said softly, and then whispered his own love against her lips. They lay for a time, drifting in comfortable companionship.

They might have fallen asleep, but eventually, Isobel stirred. "How goes the rest of the world?" she murmured.

"It's suffering from the absence of your brilliant mind."

"You hardly have to charm me, Riot. You've already seduced me. Thoroughly."

"I plan on seducing you daily," he said.

"You can certainly try."

Riot propped himself up with an elbow. "The rest of the world is getting along as usual, but I feel your absence keenly," he admitted. Riot felt a pang of guilt. He had his freedom. Isobel was the one confined. The asylum was far from harsh, but it was still a prison. No matter the space, a tiger still paced its cage. "I'm sorry," Riot said. "I…"

Isobel turned to face him, interlacing her fingers with his. He studied the complexity in her eyes, marveling over how sunlight turned their gray to a misty silver. "Don't apologize for missing me. *I'd* miss me," she said flippantly.

"I do. Very much." He brought their hands to his lips. "I want to drop everything and move into the cottage next door."

"You'd have to attend talking sessions," she said with a sigh.

Riot chuckled. "*How* is life without Lotario here?"

"Presently? Life is wonderful." She smiled, tugging on his beard. "But I've had to dutifully attend every single talking session. Doctor Bright and I have established what I already knew—that I'm impatient, don't suffer fools, and I got in over my head with the whole… Kingston affair. At the very least, my talking sessions seem to make Julius feel better."

"But not you?" he asked.

She raised a brow in a kind of shrug. "*You* make me feel better. I'm at peace when I'm with you. I feel… whole."

"I know the feeling, which is strange considering I've lived most my life without you."

"I only have seventy days left." It seemed like an eternity. Isobel took a breath. "It could be worse. And Julius and I are… friends now. It's the only way I agreed to talk with him."

"As perceptive as you are, I doubt he had little choice in the matter. It was either befriend you or live with the knowledge that a patient had walked away with all his secrets."

"Well, there is that." Another smile, and she untangled herself, heading for the bathroom. Riot reached for his spectacles, so he might watch her walk. Sleek muscle, power, and grace. And laughter. She shut the door on his appreciative gaze.

Riot reached for their clothes on the floor, sorting them, and laying them over a chair. He frowned at the creases in his trousers. Hopefully no one at the asylum was as perceptive as Isobel. He poured water into a basin from a pitcher, and inspected himself in the mirror. The signs were obvious to him: worn out, supremely relaxed and unaccountably content. And that tilt to his shoulders. It shouted of a man who had just made love to the satisfaction of both parties.

Riot dunked his head in the water, and smoothed his hair. When he reached for a towel, he heard the door open, and felt eyes on his back. "Did you have time to check on Lotario?"

"Didn't you receive my telegram?"

"'Your reflection is lovely' isn't very reassuring."

"Lotario is fine," Riot assured.

"Where is he?"

"In the area."

"You're being vague, Riot." Her voice neared, and then her body. Breasts pressed against his back and he forgot what they had been talking about. Isobel traced the muscles of his backside. "I still haven't seen you fence," she murmured.

Her touch rekindled his desire.

"My performance is far from spectacular," he said, meeting her eyes in the mirror.

"Your physique says otherwise."

To give himself time, Riot dried his face on a towel. It was enough, barely. "Are you attempting to seduce me for information?" he asked, suddenly.

"I only want to know what my twin is up to."

Riot set down the towel, and turned, casually leaning against the washstand. "Lotario accused you of sending me to spy on him."

"I'm not spying," she said.

Riot ran his hands up her arms. "He's in fine spirits. Trust me. He made me swear to tell you nothing more."

"Are you taking sides?"

"Only honoring his request."

"What of mine?" she asked.

"You only asked me to check on him, Bel." Riot leaned forward to kiss her again, but she slipped to the side. She had that calculating look about her. Before she came to a conclusion (which she would, given enough time), Riot tossed her something else to chew on. "Have you thought about our wedding?"

"Having second thoughts?"

"Never," Riot grunted, reaching for his clothes. "Call it impatience."

Her brows shot upwards. "You? Atticus Riot, *impatient*. Where is the man I thought I knew?"

"Obscenely content at the moment." He had just got his drawers on, and was reaching for an undershirt, when Isobel closed in on him. She placed a hand on his chest, and applied pressure until the back of his knees hit the edge of the bed. He sat.

"Now I'm curious why you changed the subject, Riot."

"I was hoping my backside would be adequate distraction."

"Nearly." Isobel edged closer, straddling one of his legs.

"By all means, keep trying, Bel."

"What?" she asked innocently.

"I do enjoy being seduced by you."

"Is it working?"

Riot took a moment to appreciate the display of flesh before him. Then he looked her in the eye. "On a lesser man…"

"I wouldn't be marrying a lesser man."

"There's the catch." He slapped her flank, and she jumped in surprise. The look he received made him grin.

"I suppose you're well used to seduction," she said. "A pity." Isobel bent at the waist to retrieve her bloomers. His cocky grin fell.

Clothes rustled, and she turned, fully covered. Her eyes drifted downwards, and she arched a brow at his body's firm betrayal.

"I, er… What were we talking about?" he said, shifting into a more comfortable position. Although truth be told, nothing was currently comfortable. Only single-minded.

"Our wedding."

Her answer brought him back, and he focused on her face. Isobel had a pleased look about her—a look of triumph.

Riot reached for his trousers. "Have you thought about the ceremony? When and where you'd like to have it?"

"Will you think me cruel and uncaring if I tell you that I don't give a jot about the details. Only that you're there."

Riot took her hand. "I don't think you uncaring."

"My mother has been nagging me to have a proper church wedding at St. Mary's."

"Do you want that?" he asked.

Isobel squeezed his hand, then let go, reaching for her blouse. "I've had one. It was dreadful." She paused at her buttons. "Are you religious?"

Riot glanced at the tangled bed sheets. "Do I strike you as such?"

"That doesn't stop most people from claiming they are. Does a church wedding matter to you?" she asked.

"I've investigated too many murders and attended too many inquests to consider the buildings as divine. I'm sure Tim has a preacher friend in his pocket who'd marry us for a bottle of whiskey."

The idea clearly amused her. "We could marry here," she said. "A drunk preacher marrying a crazed convict and a gambler in an asylum. It'd almost be worth it just to see the look on my mother's face."

Riot took his time answering as he dressed. "It may not be the best for Sarah and Jin."

Isobel frowned.

"Our reputation affects them, Bel."

Concern furrowed her brow. "I see. Then we'll marry as soon as I'm free. We can march to the closest courthouse and be done with it."

Be done with it. Riot frowned at her words.

"Riot?"

He looked up.

"Did I hurt you? I didn't mean anything…"

Riot shook his head, focusing on threading a cufflink through its hole.

"You want something more, don't you?" she asked.

"Silly, isn't it?" he said. "But I think I do."

Isobel stepped up to him, and touched his temple, smoothing the streak of white hair over a deep scar along his skull. "What do you want?" she asked.

"You," he whispered.

"You have me," she said.

Her fingers dropped to his wrists, and she helped him with his cufflinks, letting him gather his words. Isobel might be impatient with others, but she always gave him time.

"I've never done anything proper in my life, Bel," he finally said. "For this, our wedding, I'd like to do it right."

Isobel glanced pointedly at the bed. "I think we're doing things a bit out of order."

"I'm only a man."

"A very good one." She kissed his cheek. "You will have your proper wedding. When I'm free. I'll even wear white. But it doesn't matter to me, so long as I do it with you."

Riot started to draw her closer, his hand curling around her waist, when a bang jerked him out of the moment. A door. Footsteps hurried across the cottage sitting room, and Riot yanked his revolver out of its holster on the chair. Vision narrowed, ears thrummed with a rush of blood, and every nerve in his body prepared for a fight.

Isobel put a hand over his. Her touch said everything, and his body trusted her instincts. Riot lowered his revolver.

"Isobel!" Sarah's voice called through the door. "Are you in there?"

Riot started for the door, but Isobel yanked him back with a hiss. She gestured at his attire. He wasn't fit to be seen, especially in a lady's bedroom.

"One moment," Isobel called lightly. "I was just resting." She gathered the remainder of his clothes, and shoved them into his arms. "What is it?"

"I couldn't find Atticus, I'm sorry. Jin's gone off to find the bear. She intends to tame it. It's all my fault. I told her about a neighbor boy who used to ride his pet bear."

Riot paused at the sill, one leg out, one leg in.

"I'll be right out. Wait in the sitting room." Isobel turned to him, and hurried over, reaching to close the shutters. "I've changed my mind," she whispered. "I *do* have a request: that we send our daughters to my mother's for our wedding trip."

DAY 57

ON THE FRINGE

Thursday, August 2 1900

"It's just 'round this way," Tim said.

Riot followed the spry old man out of the financial district towards meaner streets. They passed *Steed and Peel*, Riot's tailor, and walked one street farther, flirting with the Barbary Coast.

The street was drab and sleepy, but that would change at night.

Tim stopped at a corner and proudly gestured towards a rundown brick building. It was flanked by a cobbler and a hole-in-the-wall Italian restaurant. Riot looked down the next street.

"There's a whore house on the next block," Riot said.

"One of the more discreet ones," Tim defended. "And there's a post office, cafe, and telegraph office the other way. Look, A.J., you wanted cheap. I found you cheap."

The doorway was boarded up, and the remnants of adverts for whiskey, bawdy shows, and plays were plastered over the broken windows. "A saloon?" Riot asked.

"Eh." Tim tilted his hand this way and that. "They sold liquor."

"It was a brothel," Riot concluded.

"It's been awhile," Tim said. "Ol' Bessy was renting out rooms, and stashed enough to retire to the country somewhere. I got a steal on it."

Small wonder judging from the state of disrepair. It wasn't a large building, but Ravenwood Agency didn't need large. Only practical. Riot walked to the front door, and Tim handed him a key, but there was no lock, only boards. Riot tested a corner, and pried it easily away. "There'll be squatters inside," he surmised.

Riot set the board aside and a stench assaulted him: musty stillness and rotting food with a dash of human waste.

Tim placed a hand on the bowie knife sheathed at his waist. He'd have a sawed-off shotgun under his long coat, too. Riot ducked under the boards, and stepped inside. A patch of sunlight shone through the makeshift door, but the rest of the room was dark.

"Hello there," Riot called, holding the neck of his walking stick loosely. Noise echoed in the hollow space. Skittering, and a shift of wood. Rats. Not promising with the plague threatening the city. "Let's contact Doctor Kellogg at the Health Department. See if you can get one of his crews to disinfect."

"Will do," Tim said. Riot listened to his companion's light footsteps, then a moment later heard paper rip. Light streamed in from where Tim had peeled away an advert.

Sunlight proved too frightening for the bolder of rats as they skittered towards the backroom. It appeared that the establishment had been the scene of a roaring brawl, and the owners had simply abandoned it rather than setting things right. One lone chair stood victorious amid broken glass and wreckage.

Tim moved to a wall. "Maybe I can get one of these to work."

Riot eyed the ancient fixtures. Most had been ripped off the wall and likely salvaged. The only remaining one was bent at an odd angle.

"Doubtful."

Tim grunted, and Riot thumbed his handheld light. A weak beam shone over a battered counter. His image, dimly reflected in a broken mirror behind the bar, was splintered into a thousand fine cracks.

Tim grabbed a broken table leg, wrapped a kerchief around the end, and doused it with his flask.

"Try not to burn the city down."

"Wouldn't be the first time," Tim cackled.

"The problem is, I'm not sure if you're jesting or not."

Tim struck a match. "No faith in your elders, boy." An explosion of flame singed the man's beard, and he thrust the torch away, patting out the flames with his hand.

Burnt hair didn't help the stench.

The two moved down the hallway.

"So, uhm, when are you and Miss Bel making things official?" Tim asked.

Riot turned away from a lavatory tucked under a stairway.

"Looking forward to it that much, aye?" Tim asked, noting the look on Riot's face.

Riot pointedly closed what was left of the door on the source of the stench. Squatters weren't particular about working plumbing. "Is this really the time, Tim?"

"Just wondering."

"Bel won't be released until September."

"*And?*"

"And… she's in an asylum serving jail time." The back door was boarded up, and he pulled at the wood, but it proved solid.

"Testy, ain't you?"

Riot clenched his jaw. Thrown into yet another case, he hadn't seen Isobel in the nearly two weeks since she'd gone sprinting after Jin, who was heading for a bear cave. (What other woman would race miles to catch a child about to confront a bear?) Riot missed her quick mind. Her insight. Her energy. Her body. Yes, he was testy. Maybe he ought to move the offices to Calistoga.

"Bel was dealt a bad hand." He stifled an urge to kick the wood until it splintered. Injustice always got under Riot's skin. Instead, he moved upstairs.

"She was," Tim agreed. "But it's nearly over, and it could have been worse. Are you having a church wedding?"

"I don't know," Riot admitted. Time was dwindling, and he hadn't come up with any plans. There hadn't been time, and he still hadn't decided on a ring. "I doubt a church would take us."

Tim chuckled. "You two don't seem the type to scrape and pay for forgiveness."

"There is that."

"So what's the hold up?"

"Have you gone deaf, Tim?" Riot took the stairs two at a time. Tim kept up easily. The man was uncanny for his age.

The second story was small, two rooms for entertaining and—

A shadow in the corner stirred, a heap of rags climbing to its feet. Livid eyes pinned Riot, and a snarl struck him a second later. "Git out! Git out!" the creature screeched. The rags charged him, steel flashing. Riot stepped to the side, catching the blade on his walking stick. With a twist, he sent the knife skittering across the room. He stuck out his foot, and the ragged creature fell back to the floor.

It scrambled up, snatching at the knife, and prepared for another charge.

"Whoa, now!" Tim leveled a sawed-off shotgun at the squatter.

The heap of rags froze. Riot could just make out a snatch of gray hair framing a grimy face.

"We bought this place. You're trespassing," Tim explained.

"It's my home!" The voice, the build… Riot surmised it was

an old woman. A rat scurried out of a corner to climb up her leg and perch on her shoulder.

"Worked for Ol' Bessy, did you?" Tim asked.

The woman spat. "I ain't no whore."

"Damn straight. No whore would keep herself in such a state." Tim's words earned him a hiss and the wave of a blade.

"Madame, we're not here to hurt you. We just want our property vacated," Riot said.

"Prettified gentry."

Riot sidestepped a wad of spit. "Most call me Atticus Riot," he said with a tip of his hat.

The vagrant paused, then squinted. She looked back to Tim. "Think you're so high and mighty with that stubby little gun." The woman stepped towards Tim, pressing her forehead against the end of the barrel. "Go on, then. Blow what brains I have left."

"We ain't here to kill you," Tim said.

"I'm good as dead if you drive me out."

Tim cursed under his breath, and tucked his shotgun back under his overcoat. Clearly the woman wasn't intimidated by it.

Riot inspected the room with a sweep of eyes. Unlike the rest of the place, it was relatively clean. "Have you been chasing off the other squatters?" he asked calmly.

"I told you. It's *my* home."

"The deed I bought from Ol' Bessy says otherwise," Tim said.

"That dirty, rotten, double-crossing whore took my share and ran off."

"I thought you said you weren't a whore," Tim retorted.

"I ain't!"

Before the two could get into a lengthy argument—Tim would argue with a mule—Riot asked after her name.

She told him he could leave in the crudest of terms.

"It's a pleasure to meet you, Miss Off," Riot said, unfazed.

The woman gave a laugh. The kind that skimmed madness.

"There's three ways we could proceed," he continued, raising his fingers. "I'll give you five dollars to vacate the property. We'll summon the police." Another wad of spittle. "Or, I'll pay you five dollars a week, plus room and board, to clean our office and guard it at night once you make yourself presentable."

Tim rolled his eyes at the offer.

"Give me the money," Miss Off demanded.

Riot got out his billfold and handed over a bill. She snatched it, gathered her meager belongings without complaint, and they watched her scramble out onto a fire escape.

"Are you mad?" Tim asked.

Riot swept his stick towards the vacated room. "Say what you will, but she kept this room clean."

Tim stroked his beard. "It wouldn't live up to Miss Lily's standards."

"Neither do you, but Miss Lily still lets you inside the house."

"I know how to clean up," Tim huffed.

"Miss Lily's trained you well. Never thought it would be possible for an old dog like you."

"God's bones, don't talk like that, boy."

"That's more like it," Riot said.

"So what do you think?" Tim asked.

"It has potential," Riot said. "It's well situated. Welcoming to the fringes of society like ourselves, and yet not too far out of respectable territory."

"Not the office. That's settled whether you like it or not. I'm asking after your wedding."

"Tim, I've explained it. Bel's incarcerated."

Tim flicked the back of Riot's hat. "In a damn pleasure resort."

Riot readjusted his hat, and stepped away.

"Look, I know a preacher who'll marry anyone for a bottle of whiskey."

Riot knew Tim too well. It was exactly what Riot had told Isobel. "Why are you so eager to marry me off?"

Tim scratched his beard. "Just want to see it done."

"Afraid I'll get cold feet?"

"No, I'm afraid *I'll* get cold feet in a grave, boy."

"You're too stubborn to die." It was said lightly, but Riot had to force his tone.

"Afraid it's not entirely up to me, now is it?" Tim replied. Riot took the question as rhetorical. "But what is up to me, is getting this place in order and seeing you married. What I don't get is why you're waiting."

Riot tapped his walking stick against his shoulder. "I don't have a ring," he admitted. "And… I want to do right by Bel. I want to do something halfway decent for once. She deserves more than a soaked preacher in an asylum."

"Then make it happen, boy. Shanghai a damn priest and a wedding party if you have to."

Shanghai. The word stuck in Riot's mind, nudging his memory. An idea began to form as Tim stomped off to explore the rest of the building.

A head poked from the rear window, gray hair hanging down like a wire brush. "Ain't that just so sweet, dullard. If you want my opinion, that woman would be better off running from a shaney like you."

"Then why haven't *you* run?" Riot asked.

The woman dug in her bodice, and dropped the five dollar bill on the floor. "I changed my mind. I'll take your third offer."

"If we're going to do business together, I'll need your name," Riot said.

"Miss *Off*. Lucky Off." It was close enough.

DAY 20

SAYING GOODBYE

Sunday, September 9 1900

SUNLIGHT STREAMED THROUGH A WINDOW AT THE END OF THE attic. Swirling dust motes danced in its light, but the air smelled of stale memories. The floorboards creaked under Riot's feet as he weaved through the detritus of life—journals and personal belongings that had never been returned to their crates after the harried events of past months. Ravenwood's life had been stuffed into an attic, and now it was about to be placed in a basement or end in a rubbish bin.

Riot frowned at the darkness. So foreboding. Was it right to *stuff* a child up here? Even though Jin had readily agreed to moving into the attic, Riot was having second thoughts now that he stood in the dark space.

Sarah breezed past him with a bucket. A kerchief kept her black hair in place, and an apron protected her dress. She walked on her tip toes, something she did whenever she was excited. She headed straight for the window, dunked a rag, and started cleaning the glass. Sharp scents of lemon and vinegar chased away the staleness in the air. New life. And fresh light as the grime was washed away.

"I wouldn't mind staying up here," Sarah said as she worked. "Jin can take the other room."

"*You* can have my room. I'll take this one. We don't even have to clean it," Tobias said, from where he leaned against the railing.

"You're just trying to get out of cleaning," Sarah said.

"No matter who gets the attic room we're still cleaning it," Riot said, rolling up his shirtsleeves. A part of him wanted to sort Ravenwood's things alone, while another part was glad for company.

Riot lit the lone gas lamp as Tobias dragged broom and dustpan across the planks like a soldier marching to his doom.

Light chased back shadows and Sarah opened a pane in the attic window to let in fresh air. The small opening, and the flickering gas lamp brought an uncomfortable thought to Riot's mind—fire. The attic was a good four stories high. Anyone up here would be trapped on the roof. Riot opened the roof hatch, and climbed up a short iron ladder.

He stepped onto a small flat section of roof that was ringed by an iron-wrought parapet that barely reached his knees. Tobias poked his head out the hatch, and started to climb onto the roof. Riot held out a hand. "Stay back. We're a good four stories up."

Tobias ignored him, and climbed out anyway. "I've been up here before."

"That's what I'm worried about." Riot tested the short railing. It was anchored securely. He could hang a rope ladder from it for emergencies. It would be safer than the drain pipes.

"How come Sarah has to go to school while Jin is living it up at a resort?" Tobias asked, standing right at the edge of the railing to look down. Riot stifled an urge to grab the boy. Although Riot tolerated heights well enough, he had never been comfortable. And when a child was involved, well that made him downright queasy. Riot focused on the view. It was extraordinary. All of San Francisco was laid at their feet with the ocean on three sides.

"So, how come we have to be taught by Miss Dupree?"

"Because Jin had the sense to run away," Riot replied without thinking.

"Are you telling me to run away?"

"Only stating a fact."

Below, Tim and Grimm were brushing down the horses, and a trio of small yipping dogs ran circles in a neighbor's yard. Maybe this *was* the perfect place for Jin. High enough above the city that she'd never feel trapped again. Especially with a rope ladder.

Riot turned to find Tobias staring thoughtfully at his forearm, where a worn dragon tattoo spiraled along the skin.

"I'm not sure Jin is enjoying her respite," Riot said.

"Why's that?"

"Because Bel is teaching her."

Tobias made a face.

"Not keen on that either?

"My ma would warn me to keep my lips sealed, sir."

"Smart lad."

"Where'd you get that tattoo?"

"In Shanghai. It's a maritime tradition."

"You were a sailor?"

"No, I was young and dumb."

Riot climbed back down into the attic, and Tobias dropped down after him. The boy was springy. "Still not right she's getting out of cleaning her own room," Tobias said.

"You're getting paid," Riot pointed out.

"My ma made me put that Lady Liberty coin in the bank," Tobias said, kicking at a box. "Well, *she's* the bank."

Riot stroked his beard in contemplation. "We'll make a new deal. I'll pay you with a bag of candy."

Tobias' eyes went wide. "It's a deal." He grabbed Riot's hand and shook.

"Tobias! That's pure dumb," Sarah said.

"My ma ain't gonna let me touch my own money till I'm all grown. I'd rather eat candy now."

Sarah opened her mouth, and then closed it. The logic was infallible.

Riot dragged a crate away from the wall. "You lost your chance," he murmured to Sarah.

"For what?"

"Ask for his wages and buy the bag of candy yourself," he said for her ears alone.

A light turned on in her eyes. "Say, Tobias. I'll buy you *two* bags of candy if you hand over your wages to me."

"You think I'm an idiot? You'll give me the old, cheap stuff that the sweet shop is about to toss."

"And Atticus won't?" she returned.

Tobias glanced at Riot. "He's honest. Not double-dealing like you."

"I'm nearly a saint," Riot said, jamming a crowbar under the lid. Nails squealed as he applied pressure, and he thought he heard Sarah say, "Charm the devil himself."

Dust filled the attic, and the lid fell to the planks with a slam. They coughed and sneezed, and all eyes peered curiously into the crate. Books. More books.

Sarah picked up a book and dusted it off. She wrinkled her nose. "*Landscape Gardening*?" Not something one would expect from the legendary Zephaniah Ravenwood.

Tobias hoisted himself to look into the crate. "How come we're unpacking everything when we aim to clear it all out?"

A good question. Riot had no answer. It was more of a compulsion. A need to sort the last of Ravenwood's belongings himself.

"When my gramma died, I did the same," Sarah whispered, opening the book in her hands. "I think it was like saying goodbye."

Tobias heaved out a metal contraption from under a pile of books. "Did your gramma keep bear traps too?"

Riot quickly took the thing from Tobias. Why on earth had Ravenwood kept a trap that had been used for murder? With what appeared to be dried blood still on the teeth. Riot tried not to think of the grisly body that had been caught in the jaws, and he certainly didn't enlighten the children on its history.

"This is why we're sorting things first. I'm not keen on dumping weapons with the scavengers and ragpickers. I need to disarm the attic."

"Amen," Sarah said. "You want Jin sleeping up here with something like that on hand, Tobias?"

Tobias's eyes turned to saucers. "Oh, heck no." The boy started gathering everything from fire pokers and hatpins to pencils, and dumping them into an empty chest that he dubbed the "armory."

Four hours later a bedraggled trio carried the last of Ravenwood's earthly belongings to a basement storage room. A quarter of belongings would go to scavengers and half would go to pawnshops, while the armory found an eternal resting place in the basement. Riot made sure to lock the door, and pocket the key.

"Thank you for your help," Riot said to the children as they trudged back up the stairs.

"I'll give the attic a good sweep," Sarah said.

"We can tackle that tomorrow," he offered.

"And paint and wallpaper? A rug would be nice. What color do you reckon Jin likes?" Sarah asked.

"Crazy," Tobias said.

"That's not a color," Sarah said.

"We'll let Miss Lily decide on that," Riot said.

"Decide on what?" Miss Lily stood in the entryway, removing hat and gloves. Riot hurried over to help her with her coat.

"Thank you, Mr. Riot. Now what am I being volunteered for?"

"We were discussing decorating the attic for Jin. I was hoping for your input," Riot said.

"I wager it's the only room she's ever had. I'd suggest white-washing the wood and buying some basic furniture. Leave the rest to her."

"I never got to do that," Tobias said. "I'm stuck with all sorts of flowers."

"Well, you can whitewash Jin's room tomorrow to get a taste of what it's like," Lily said to her son. "And don't think you're getting out of school."

"I'll help you," Sarah said. "I've painted before."

"Mr. Riot, can I speak with you after you've had a chance to settle?"

"Now will do."

Miss Lily took a breath and showed him into the greenhouse, where his dusty clothes wouldn't make a mess. She didn't sit in one of the garden chairs, so he waited.

"If we're to be partners, I won't stand on ceremony. Sit if you like."

Miss Lily appeared troubled, so Riot remained standing.

"It's about your offer of partnership, and that gold."

"I didn't win that gold at the tables," he assured her.

Lily shook her head. "Tobias filled my ear with how you came by it. I don't doubt your word." She looked him square in the eye. "I'd never doubt that."

Riot nodded slowly. He thought gambling was the source of her unease. Clearly he had been wrong. He took a chair and sat, hoping it would put her at ease.

Lily straightened her cuffs, and took a breath. "Over the past few weeks, I've been watching the stock market and speaking with a number of associates about possible investments. I've narrowed down three proposals for our investment. But mind you, none of them are without risk."

"Investing is always a gamble."

"I'm glad you understand that," Lily said, inclining her head. "The first is mundane: railway, ferry, and mining prospects. The telephone companies too."

"Already heavily invested in."

She nodded. "But traditional. The second isn't."

"I'm not a traditional man, Miss Lily."

"This borders on eccentric. For a white gentleman, at any rate."

Riot waited.

"I have a friend, a chemist from Hampton University. Miss Vivian Leigh. And she's… *we* are looking for investors for a hair product company."

Riot stared, and then tilted his head. "Aren't there plenty of companies that sell that sort of thing?"

"Hair products for white folks. Not for negroes." Lily took a seat, and patted her hair. Her black hair was piled into a stylish Gibson Girl arrangement that he had seen on numerous women.

"I don't follow, Miss Lily. Why can't negroes use the same products?"

"Everyone has different textures. Some Irish have curly hair. Blonde women have very fine hair. Spanish have thicker hair. Some hair is oily, and other hair is dry. But the products on the market are harsh and ruinous for hair like mine. And that's common for folks of my color."

"I see," he said slowly. Riot hadn't given women's hair of any type much thought. There was Bel's, of course, but she tended to chop it off and dye it on a whim. He didn't much care what she did with her hair, as long she was happy doing it.

"I understand if you aren't interested in such a venture—"

"Do you think there's a market for it?" he interrupted.

"I do."

"Then that's good enough for me."

Lily looked relieved. "To be honest, I thought you'd laugh at the idea. Most gentlemen would scoff at putting their money into hair products, let alone products for negroes."

"I'm making you a partner, Miss Lily. I don't make deals with people I find comical. I make them with people I trust. You mentioned a third option?"

"I received a tip about *San Francisco Gas and Electric Company*. They're set to take the city and buy out the competition. If it happens, their stocks will soar."

"Do you trust this source?"

"On this subject, I do. It's Mrs. Mary Ellen Pleasant."

"I've heard of her."

"I'm sure you've heard a lot. Some of it's true, but most of it isn't."

Riot cracked a rueful smile. "Sounds like my memoir."

Mary Ellen Pleasant had been a force to be reckoned with a decade or two ago. Rumors abounded, and the newspapers liked to spin wild tales about the woman. If Riot were to pick threads from the rumors, it'd be that she was a shrewd business woman who made a young clerk by the name of Thomas Bell wealthy. And that she had used a network of housemaids and cooks to eavesdrop on business men. But if newspapers could be trusted, the Bell family and Mrs. Pleasant had recently had a falling out, leaving Mrs. Pleasant near to penniless.

"Mrs. Pleasant's name is in ruins, but that doesn't mean she stopped being a shrewd investor."

"With the help of her chain of informants?"

Lily only smiled. "You don't take issue with Mr. Tim's friends."

"I don't. But then he reports to me. My only concern is what this information has cost you, Miss Lily."

Lily arched a brow. "I'm half in this with you, Mr. Riot. It's in my best interest to succeed. Don't you worry about that. But she did warn me not to trust you."

"And why is that?"

"Mrs. Pleasant was ruined when Thomas Bell died. She used him as a front to carry out business in his name. Something she couldn't freely do as a negro woman. The trouble was, she didn't have her name on things. As soon as he died, and people learned she was the real power behind the Bell's wealth. Well… she became a target."

"I'm sure you'll have proper papers drawn up, Miss Lily."

Lily shook her head. "There's the crux. I can't have my name anywhere on this money. I can't keep a bank account. I can't own property. I can't have anything given to me in a will. And my face most definitely cannot appear in a newspaper."

Riot let her words settle. Her breath had come quicker as she'd spoken, and she held herself stiffly. But underneath, he sensed she was cracking.

Riot leaned forward. "Miss Lily," he said softly. "Who's after you?"

Her lips only formed a tight line.

"I told you about my half-sister because you told me it seemed like something you ought to know. I think the same applies here," he said.

Lily shook her head. "Trust me. It's not the same. All you need to know is that one day you may find me and mine gone. I'll keep my share of the money in your safe, if that's agreeable. And I'll take it when we leave."

The thought of Ravenwood Manor without the White family disturbed him. He started to argue, but she held up a hand.

"I wouldn't do so out of any willingness, or ill feelings against you or your household. I hope that day never comes, Mr. Riot, but with my luck, it will. And the less you know the better."

Riot held her eyes, curiosity burning in his mind. Did this business have something to do with Grimm and his selective muteness? Was she protecting her son? But Riot didn't press her. Some things were better left buried, and he hoped it stayed that way. "I think Mrs. Pleasant is right to be distrustful. That's putting a lot of faith in me. Question is… do you trust me with that sort of arrangement?" He held out a hand.

But instead of a simple shake, Lily placed her hand in his. "I do, Mr. Riot." She squeezed it, and then let go.

"Then invest our hard-earned gold," he said. "I like the hair product venture. Ravenwood would have had an apoplectic seizure knowing his money was tied up in women's hair products. Take what's left and put it in the electric company."

Lily nodded. "I was going to suggest that very thing."

"But, Miss Lily. If I ever wake up to find your family gone, you can be assured I'll not let it rest."

"I wish you would, Mr. Riot. You may not like what you stir up."

He gave her a small smile. "That's never stopped me before."

They rose, and he opened the greenhouse door for her. "Miss Lily?"

She paused. "Yes?"

"I forgot all about that safe. Is there anything of Ravenwood's in there, aside from his money?"

"There's a wooden box in the back."

"What's in the box?" Riot asked.

"I don't know. There's no keyhole or lid."

A LONE MAN SAT IN THE LIBRARY OF RAVENWOOD MANOR, hunched and snoring with an electric-blue book on his expansive gut. The glass on the table beside him looked more like whiskey than water.

Riot had seen the boarder only in passing. A Mr. Dougal? No, that was another boarder with a laugh like a canon boom. This was… Did it matter? Riot wondered how many boarders Ravenwood Manor had.

Riot sat down in an armchair opposite, and took out his deck of cards. He squared his favored deck, and then began to shuffle. A flurry of cards passed from hand to hand with methodical rhythm. He had been thrown into one thing after another since arriving in San Francisco's port, and hadn't thought about checking Ravenwood's safe. He had forgotten it even existed.

Riot watched the man across from him with piercing eyes. He increased the range and speed of his shuffling, and eventually the frenetic pace disturbed the peace.

The boarder's eyes flew open. Riot nodded to the man. Hughes. That was the name: Harry Hughes. Riot was rather glad he had been able to choose his own name. What if he had ended up as an Andy Apple?

"Oh, er… Mr. Riot. I was just reading."

"I come here for the quiet too," Riot said, his voice low and his gaze steady. The cards never faltered.

Hughes shifted, looking around uncomfortably. "Yes, yes, I'll leave you to it, then." He stood hastily, his book sliding to the floor.

"No need," Riot said easily.

"I should find my bed. Perhaps we can have a drink sometime."

Riot inclined his head, and the man swayed from the library. He waited for the door to close, and squared his deck, tucking it away. He plucked up the forgotten book: *Hints to Lady Travellers*. Unexpected. Keeping an ear cocked towards the door, Riot restored the book to its resting place, and turned to another bookcase.

He ran a finger along the titles until he found *A Treatise on Safe Cracking and Locks*. Ravenwood did like his little jokes. Riot pulled the book, and a soft click indicated a latch was triggered. The bookcase swung outward, shelves and all. A heavy iron safe sat squarely in the center.

Riot turned the dial. 07. 23. 44. Right, left, and right. The numbers had always made him curious. Were they random? Or a date? Ravenwood was born in 1822, so it wasn't his birthdate. But was it someone else's? Riot wrenched the handle and the safe cracked open. A neat pile of gold coins and cash sat inside, along with an emerald necklace.

Riot carefully shifted the piles, and reached all the way into the back, where a wooden box was lost in shadow. Riot dragged it out and closed the safe, sliding the bookshelf back in place. He sat down and set the decorative box on his lap. Edelweiss blossoms were carved on the top. Miss Lily had been correct. There was no discernible lid or lock.

Riot closed his eyes, and explored the contours of the wood with his fingertips. Lock picking and cards required a sensitivity that Riot had honed over the years. He nudged a carving to the side, and pulled at another segment of wood. A key fell into his palm. Riot slid the pieces back in place, and turned the box around. With both hands he pressed at the main part of the box. A slot opened, and he inserted the key and turned it. *Click*.

Ravenwood had been a vexing puzzle of a man, and Riot had been so irritated with him that emotion had squashed his curiosity. He hadn't wanted to delve into Ravenwood's past, nor had Ravenwood wanted him to. The secretive man had valued his privacy.

Riot opened the lid and stared at the contents for a long minute. This was private. Most definitely private. Riot shut the box and considered. Did he have a right to invade a dead man's secrets?

Was this an invasion of privacy, or was it closure?

I leave a son, the words written in Ravenwood's journal came unbidden. They were burned into Riot's mind's eye, a voice from the grave granting him permission. Riot opened the box again.

He reached inside, and picked out a framed picture. It was a painted portrait of a woman—a handsome woman with curly red hair piled high on her head. There was intelligence in those eyes. A lock of vibrant red hair tied with a green bow lay next to it. He touched the hair, and then quickly drew back. A lock of hair signified intimacy—it wasn't given lightly to a gentleman of that era.

Riot checked the back of the picture. *Beatrix, 1872*. Three years before Ravenwood came to America. Riot turned to the other item in the box: a gold ring on a chain.

DAY 0

FREEDOM

Saturday, September 29 1900

ISOBEL STARED AT HER WATCH AS SECONDS TICKED BY. FIVE minutes. Another rotation. A click, and the long hand edged closer to the number twelve.

Why did time move so slowly when observed?

She felt a child again, trapped in a classroom. Her parents had abandoned the notion of formal schooling after she climbed out a window during class, to follow a hawk. Lotario had followed too, of course. But no amount of discipline, reasoning, or time in a corner wearing a dunce hat ever deterred Isobel Amsel. She simply walked off, or dug in her heels and kept poking at the disciplinaries to see how far she could drive them. As it turned out, she could drive an adult fairly far.

Ten, nine, eight, Isobel held her breath. *Seven, six, five, four, three*, what would freedom feel like after a year? *Two, one*, the long hand clicked to the right, covering the short hand. Midnight.

The seconds ticked on, and Isobel stared at her watch. The world kept spinning.

She sat in an empty room, alone. And wept. A silent shuddering release. It was finally over. Kingston. Her cruel brother Curtis and his conspiracies. The trial. It was over. She was finally free to live her life—to run away, to strike out across the world and leave this mess. If she wanted to.

Isobel scraped a palm across her eyes, and blinked at the darkness. Then at her watch. Fifteen minutes of freedom and she had wasted it on a maudlin display of emotion. Insufferable.

Isobel stood up, slapped a hat on her head, slung a coat over her arm, and snatched up her suitcase to march into the adjoining room.

Jin slept in a cot, the scars that crisscrossed her face stark in the moonlight. And yet, Jin slept so peacefully. Bright Waters had been therapeutic for the child. Isobel shook the girl's shoulder. Jin shot out of the blanket, rolled to the side, and came up in a crouch, nostrils flaring.

"I love how quickly you get out of bed," Isobel said, impressed. "Come on, get dressed."

"What is the matter?" Jin asked, searching the room for threat.

Isobel let her watch dangle on its chain. "I'm free. It's time to go."

Jin blew an annoyed breath past her lips. "It is night. Atticus is coming this afternoon."

It was true. That was the plan, at any rate. Another case had taken him away these past weeks, but he and Sarah were set to arrive this afternoon and travel back with them the next day.

"I do not want to spend another day here," Isobel said.

Jin cursed under her breath. "We might miss Atticus and Sarah."

Isobel had already thought of that. "Not if we catch the first train."

"What if *he* catches the first train?"

"I want to surprise him," Isobel returned.

"What if he was going to surprise you?" Jin shouted the question. "Let me go back to sleep!"

Isobel took a steadying breath, closed her eyes, and exhaled. When she opened her eyes, Jin was still glaring up at her defiantly. She doubted another calming breath would fix the girl's scowl.

"You may remain here if you like. I'm free. You're free. We can do whatever the hell we like. And I'm leaving." Isobel felt elated.

Resigned, Jin yanked on her clothes: loose shirt, trousers, and an oversized cap that she tucked her braids under. Isobel tossed the girl's meager belongings into a rucksack, and slung it over a shoulder.

Jin trudged sleepily in her wake as they exited the cottage. "Are we going to walk the whole way?" Jin asked.

Crickets and frogs made the night alive, and the moon lit their feet. "You've been a ball of energy these past three months, and *now* you want to laze around in bed snoring?"

"I do not snore. You do."

"Just imagine how glorious it will be when you won't have to listen to me snore anymore. So stop dragging your feet."

This only made Jin walk slower. The girl looked at her feet, shuffling them along the dirt. "You will be too busy for me now."

"Nonsense." But Jin was likely right. As a girl, Isobel had hated lying adults, and here she was dispensing false assurances.

Isobel stopped, and knelt in front of Jin, looking her in the eye. "You're right, Jin. Things will be hectic, but you'll be a part of that hectic life, and I'll be a part of yours. And Sarah's, and Riot's, and Tim's, and even my parents. Life gets busy when you have family."

Isobel pulled the girl into a hug, and Jin held on fiercely. "Thanks for keeping me company," Isobel whispered.

"It was not too bad."

Isobel held her at arm's length. "Me or Bright Waters?"

Jin bared her white teeth in the dark. In reply, Isobel flicked the tip of her cap, and stood, heading towards the main ward.

The nurses kept the doors locked, but if there was one thing Isobel had had, it was time—time to perfect her lock-picking and time to perfect her pickpocketing. The nurses made for excellent marks. Isobel removed a stolen key from her pocket and inserted it in the lock. She ushered Jin inside the ward, and carefully closed the door.

Their footsteps echoed softly in the entryway, and from somewhere distant, a patient cried out in the night. That would be Freddie. The soldier had returned from the Philippines, but his mind was still on a distant battlefield. Isobel had helped Julius make some progress with him. She had taken him on long walks, and didn't push him for conversation or demand anything of the soldier. Enough had already been asked of him.

Isobel and Jin climbed the stairs, and walked to Julius's door. Not his consultation room, but his private rooms. She knocked. It felt wrong to leave without saying farewell to the alienist. She certainly never intended to return.

Jin shifted at her side, gazing down the empty corridor. The child edged closer, and Isobel put an arm around her slight shoulders. The girl no longer flinched or growled when Isobel touched her. The months here had calmed Jin, or maybe Isobel had finally earned her full trust.

Isobel knocked again. Louder. It boomed down the hallway. A door opened, but not the one Isobel wanted. The head nurse poked her head into the hallway, and a light flicked on. "Miss Amsel!"

Isobel cleared her throat. It was Miss Floyd, the hair puller.

"What on earth are you doing?" Miss Floyd demanded. She marched towards them, in nightcap and robe.

"I'm knocking on a door," Isobel explained.

"Get back to your rooms. How did you get in here?"

Isobel held up her watch on its chain. "I'm no longer confined here. I don't have to listen to you anymore."

Miss Floyd made an exasperated noise. "As if you ever did! Can't you just leave quietly?"

"We intend to. As soon as I say goodbye to Dr. Bright."

The woman's face lit with joy. "How delightful you're leaving. But I'm afraid Dr. Bright went away on business. He won't be back for three days."

Isobel felt a sinking in the pit of her stomach. "He didn't tell me."

"You're a patient, Miss Amsel." And then she brightened once again. "*Were.*"

"Can you see to my trunks?"

"Of course. Goodbye. Do give your brother my warmest regards. I do hope he is doing well." Miss Floyd walked back to her rooms and shut the door.

Isobel stared at the emptiness, feeling an unexpected disappointment. But then what had she expected? A midnight celebration?

"Nurse Floyd seems very happy," Jin noted.

Isobel nodded, absently picking up her suitcase. "We definitely left an impression on her." They walked through the empty hallways and into the night. Isobel spotted Gus, the night guard, sleeping by a fountain. She gestured Jin to stay back, and crept forward. The man continued snoring as she dropped her stolen key into his breast pocket. There. That was done.

As he coughed and muttered, Isobel hurried back to Jin, and the two slipped away into the sleepy night, and down a long, lonely road.

"Are we walking all the way to the train?" Jin whispered.

"It's only a few miles or so."

"The first train does not leave until six-thirty."

Isobel smiled. "I know."

"It is dark out."

"It's practically bright. Look at the stars, Jin. *Smell* the earth."

"And listen to the coyotes. The nurses say there is a roaming pack of starving coyotes that eat people who leave the asylum."

"Nonsense. I've only heard one coyote tonight."

"And crickets," Jin said.

"Are you afraid of crickets?"

"I do not trust them," the girl said. She quickened her pace, nearly running to catch up. "Have you taken cocaine?"

Isobel looked down at the girl. "Why would you think that?"

"You are very happy. The women at the brothels would sometimes take the white powder. Mei told me to stay away from it."

"I concur. And no, I'm not on cocaine." Though she had tried it. "I'm *free*!"

"You weren't a very good captive."

Isobel refused to be drawn into a debate with a ten-year-old child. "You're free too."

"I will have to go to school."

"You like school."

"When it's not boring," Jin said.

"Aren't you excited to see your new room?"

Jin didn't answer. It was admittance enough that she was, at the very least, intrigued. "I think we should wait for Atticus," Jin said after a stretch.

"Noted," Isobel growled through her teeth. Apparently she was the only person excited over her release.

They walked in silence down the secluded road. The heat of the previous day rose from the earth while mist worked its sinuous way down hillsides to fill the valley. With every step, Isobel felt lighter. A weight lifted that had become so familiar she had forgotten it was there.

An hour later, Isobel stood at the entrance to a dark town. The only noise came from a lit saloon, and even that was winding down. A drunk man slurred a greeting, as they walked through town towards the train station. A single lamp lit the closed ticket booth.

"Now what?" Jin asked.

Isobel stared at the dark tracks. Thirty-seven miles to Vallejo ferry terminal. Isobel had a quick stride, and she managed about four miles an hour. Too long. But if she ran… Isobel glanced at Jin. Maybe a horse? With what money, came the next thought. She only had enough for the train, ferry, and maybe a meal for the two of them.

Resigned, Isobel sat on a bench and consulted her watch. Three hours to go. "We'll wait."

Jin blew out a breath, dropped her rucksack, and climbed onto the bench. She curled into a ball, resting her head on Isobel's thigh. Isobel draped her coat over the girl.

Three hours. But it would be three hours of freedom. Choice. What a precious thing, to simply *be* in a place of one's own choosing. That made the wait more than tolerable.

DREAMS

At five-thirty in the morning, a short, round man in a bowler walked onto the train platform. Isobel dislodged Jin, whose head fell to the bench with a clunk. Isobel winced, and made a mental note that children slept like bricks, then reassured herself that children were far more durable than they appeared.

Isobel headed straight for the stationmaster's office, and drummed her fingers impatiently on the ledge.

"That's not going to make the train come any sooner, Miss," the man called from inside. A latch clicked, and the ticket window opened. The round man now wore a stationmaster's hat and a clerk's sleeves.

Isobel pushed coins at him. "Two tickets to Vallejo."

"Been here all night, have you? Running from trouble?"

"I never run from trouble," she replied.

The man stared a moment, digesting her words, and then jumped to action. "I'll just open the lady's waiting room for you, Miss… erm?"

"Amsel."

"Have a safe journey, Miss Amsel." His eyes flickered to the side, to the inside wall of his booth.

"I was released today," Isobel explained. "There's no need to go scampering off to report me to Sheriff Nash."

The man started, putting on a look of pure innocence.

"It's obvious you have my likeness plastered on your wall with the rest of the 'wanted' posters."

The man cleared his throat, and left to open the waiting room for her. But Isobel wasn't about to wait in a stuffy room. She went back to her bench, and sat. Not a minute later, she heard the tapping of a telegraph. Isobel cocked an ear, deciphering the code: Miss Amsel is at the station.

Hell. Was he notifying reporters? The police? She didn't relish having an audience, or worse being hassled by police. But what if his message was being sent to one of her many enemies?

Isobel checked her watch as Jin sat up, blinking at the light. "I suppose some coffee wouldn't hurt. And biscuits."

Jin perked up at that word.

As they walked towards the cafe, the stationmaster poked his head out the window. "Uhm, Miss Amsel. Where are you going?"

Isobel didn't answer. She wanted to strangle the man.

"Why does he care where we go?"

"I suppose we'll find out eventually."

Jin glanced over her shoulder. "I do not like how he is looking at us. We should go back to the asylum."

A knot formed between Isobel's shoulders. She expected to be seized at any moment. Would her ex-husband send someone after her? Her instincts said yes, but not so soon. It would be far too obvious. Why not kill her in the asylum and make it look like a suicide?

Isobel itched for a weapon.

She sat with her back against a wall as they ate, but breakfast passed without incident and the train rolled into the station on time. The early train brought workers, and a few eager tourists. But no reporters. Isobel pulled Jin onto the train and they took their seats. The bell rang, the train chugged forward, and no one bothered them. Isobel began to relax.

Between her faked death and arrest, she realized she had been on edge for over a year. *Was* she paranoid? Probably. But was that such a bad thing?

The train soon lulled her, and she let her mind wander. She was free. She could do anything she pleased. True, she'd be married—to an amazing, dangerous man who was not only her partner but also her best friend. And she had two daughters to look after. Each adrift. But one needed a crew before setting sail. The thought brought another, and she nudged Jin with an elbow.

"Is there someplace you'd like to travel to?" Isobel asked.

Jin looked from the window. "We are traveling now." Jin's imagination had been murdered along with her parents. The girl was far too literal for a child.

"I mean somewhere else. London? New York? Hawaii?"

Jin's frown deepened. "I don't know many places."

"We'll have to change that."

"I want to sail. Like you."

Isobel nodded. "We *will* do that." Except… splitting wood and rushing water assailed her. Isobel shivered. The *Pagan Lady* had been sunk. Right. She made a mental list, practical as always: marry Riot, then repair her boat. There was the small manner of money, however. Riot had told her of his financial situation, and she was worse off than he was. Perhaps she could win a new boat at a gambling table? Surely Riot would teach her how to cheat? Did he cheat at cards? There was so much she didn't know about him. And so much she looked forward to discovering.

"I heard a man telling Mei about giant trees." Jin's voice pulled Isobel from her plotting. "I want to climb a big tree."

Isobel smiled. "Then we'll visit the big trees."

"And I want to learn to swim, and ride horses, and shoot guns. And go to Buffalo Bill's Wild West Show."

Isobel nodded. But Jin wasn't done.

"Then I want to go to London and meet Mr. Sherlock Holmes." The girl had taken to the stories with enthusiasm. Isobel hadn't had the heart to tell her that the great detective was fictional. Or that he fell off Reichenbach Falls (no matter what Riot claimed). Jin hadn't made it to "The Final Problem" yet.

Isobel gripped Jin's hand. "I don't know about the last, but we'll manage the others."

AMBUSH

Isobel stopped in her tracks at the end of the sidewalk, closed her eyes, and inhaled a deep breath through nose and mouth, both smelling and tasting the air. The stench of coal pricked her senses, and fish, but underneath, there it was, permeating everything: salt air. It energized her like a drug in her veins. The air was hot and the water glassy. She had missed this. Even the screaming seagulls circling overhead.

"Nearly there," Isobel said.

Jin looked resigned as they walked towards the crowded ferry terminal. It was prime commute time, and the line was long. Isobel stood in the queue, edging forward one person at a time.

"Two tickets for San Francisco," Isobel said, pushing coins across the counter. The ticket taker's eyes darted to the side, and he put on a large smile.

Isobel suppressed a sigh. "I was released today. Good God man, if I was actually a criminal on the run you'd likely have a gun aimed at your head. Can you be any more obvious?"

The man turned red. "I'll take your word on it, Miss Amsel." He glanced down at Jin. "Terminal two."

Isobel took the tickets, and started towards the indicated dock.

But no one else was headed that way. A group of commuters were currently boarding terminal one. Why were there two ferries in port?

She bullied her way back to the front of the line. "Shouldn't I be on the ferry that's boarding?"

"No, Miss. I gave you tickets for terminal two. The other one is full. You can board the *Tiburon* now. You don't have to wait."

Isobel narrowed her eyes. "I'm headed to San Francisco, not Sausalito.

"It's on a different schedule today."

Jin tugged on Isobel's blouse. "There are people on board," the girl said.

The man behind the counter licked his lips, and called, "Next!"

Isobel bristled, but Jin was persistent, grabbing her by the belt and tugging with all her might. "Can we just get on the ferry?" Jin asked.

"I don't like it," Isobel said. "He's hiding something."

"People are *always* hiding things," Jin said.

Children generally had the simplest and truest of insights.

"We're not getting on that ferry," Isobel whispered to the child. Instead, she gripped Jin's hand and headed for terminal one.

"I do not want to go on the crowded one."

"It's a trap, Jin."

Jin yanked her hand free, and bolted for terminal two, running straight for the open-ended aft.

"What the..." Isobel watched as Jin's cap flew off—her braids flapping behind her as she ran—and disappeared into the cavernous hold. There was nothing for it now. Steeling herself for an attack, Isobel walked towards the waiting ferry, and what was sure to be a trap. She stopped to pick up Jin's cap, and nodded to a crew member.

"Ma'am," he said, holding out a hand. She gave him their tickets, and he smiled.

Every nerve in her body screamed of danger. But he appeared genuine, wearing the customary ferryman's uniform. He was a slim fellow with rough hands from handling heavy moor lines all day. No obvious weapon, except for the common jack knife that every sailor carried. She walked out of sunlight into the dark interior.

The moment she stepped aboard, the sailor unwrapped a moor line and a horn blew. It was deafening. The smokestack billowed, and the wheel began to turn. Isobel tensed, but the sailor ignored her, going about his duties.

Isobel turned to the hold. Generally the open hold would be filled, but it was empty of wagons—a vast space with sunlight streaming from the opposite end. A lone figure stood in that warm light. The man was dressed for death, top hat and all, and had a silver walking stick.

"Riot," she breathed. Shocked and relieved, and a little irritated, she dropped her bag on deck. The two were drawn together, step by step, in a slow sort of dance. Riot tucked his hat under an arm to bow over her hand. His lips brushed her knuckles. When he straightened, he pulled her hand to his chest, and she looked up into his eyes.

"There is a deck full of disreputable society, family, and one very crotchety old man above us. Along with a retired judge," he added softly.

Isobel's voice caught in her throat. "What is this, Riot?" she finally managed.

"This *could* be a welcome home celebration." He looked at her with eyes that made her forget she was standing, or even had legs at all. "Or a wedding at sea," he whispered.

"How did you…" she cut off. "The ticket taker… No, but I

left at midnight." Her head swam. With his presence. With surprise. With the nearness of him. And joy.

Riot wrapped an arm around her waist, pulling her near. "I know you, Bel. I know you better than myself."

"Then you should know my answer."

"I'd never assume."

"Jin knew, didn't she?"

Riot nodded. "We had a wager. She didn't believe you'd leave the asylum at midnight."

Isobel snorted. "That explains so much, but… I haven't a dress." It seemed a foolish thing after she said it aloud.

"Lotario has taken care of that. He's waiting for you in the women's retiring room."

The world was spinning, and she was thankful for the support of Riot's strong arm. "I... I feel rather dizzy."

"Take your time." His voice was deep and inviting. Isobel rested her cheek against his lapels. Silk and wool filled her senses. His soft beard brushed against her forehead. He smelled of sandalwood and myrrh, and his presence calmed her. The world stopped spinning.

Isobel leaned back slightly. "You're a hopeless romantic, Riot."

"Is that a yes?"

"I'm tempted to say no just to keep from being predictable."

He smiled. A rare one that displayed his two chipped teeth. "But you won't."

"Let's get on with our lives. Together."

WILD SOULS

The engines cut off, and the ferry drifted in the San Francisco Bay. Blue-green waters sparkled under the sun. It was a lazy day—one where the wind hadn't summoned up energy to sweep through the gate. San Francisco sat on the port, Sausalito and Angel Island to starboard, and the Golden Gate waited off the bow. Gulls and sailing boats dotted the sea and sky, and salt air permeated it all.

Isobel stepped from the women's retiring room. Marcus Amsel waited outside, and he beamed at his only living daughter. He took her hands, excitement blazing in his warm blue eyes. "I like this wedding better than your last."

"I do too, father."

Tears brimmed in his eyes. "Are you ready, my little bird?" he asked in German.

In answer she kissed his cheek.

A violin played, and they walked on deck. Pomegranate boughs bloomed red, and a sea of eyes watched their entrance. Isobel searched the crowd, spotting so many familiar faces that she feared she'd need the lacy handkerchief Lotario had pressed into her hand. Some of her brothers and their families had come:

Aubert, Emmett, and Vicilia. And of course Lotario, who stood at the end of the aisle as her Man of Honor. 'Pretend I'm wearing the most gorgeous silk gown with puffed sleeves and a sleek fit,' he had whispered to her earlier, as he helped her into a simple white affair. Isobel now did, in her mind, just as he'd wished. And he was gorgeous.

Lotario's friends, the Fuzzy Bunch, had come to celebrate along with the Falcon's Bicycle Club. Isobel smiled at Margaret, who was waving from the crowd. Miss Lily and her children were in their Sunday best. Isobel's Irregulars: Miss Merrily and Mrs. Wright were present. As were Miss Meredith and Mr. Darcy, along with Julius Bright.

On Riot's side of the deck were his own friends: his agents, including Mack, Mr. Payne and Meekins, and even the reed-thin reporter, Mr. Fry. Miss Cameron was there, and Ling along with her new husband, and Dr. Wise and his family. All assembled for them. It was a motley assortment. Ragtag and rich, scoundrels and saints, standing all mixed up together. All their eyes were on her.

Isobel looked to the bow, where Tim played a violin (he gave her a wink) and Lotario, Sarah, Jin, and Tobias waited. And finally to Atticus James Riot. Calm and confident, he'd stand there for as long as she needed.

Her father stopped, just short of the end, and patted her hand, whispering, "You've always known your own mind. I'll let you walk the rest of the way on your own." He kissed her on the cheek, and went to stand with his wife. Catarina looked like a stone. She nodded to Isobel, who returned the curt gesture with one of her own.

Isobel stepped over to Riot. The violin cut off, but she barely noticed. Riot turned to face her, and took her hands. When her eyes met his, the rest of the world slipped away.

A rough throat cleared. "We are gathered here today for one

purpose: to tie these two wild souls together." The voice sounded like it had swallowed gravel for breakfast. Isobel tore her eyes from Riot's and looked at the retired judge. She blinked. A black patch covered his left eye. And when he shifted, Isobel caught a hint of silver beneath the bible in his hand. A hook. She pressed her lips together and glanced at Riot, whose eyes were dancing with the same amusement she felt. It was too much. He had found a pirate to marry them.

"I do!" she said with a laugh, throwing her arms around Riot's neck.

"Blast it, woman. We ain't there yet," the judge growled.

"I do too," Riot said.

"Wait, wait, don't start kissing," the judge ordered, putting his hook between them. "To love and to hold and all that muck?"

"Forever and always," Riot said solemnly.

"And into hell itself," Isobel added.

Her mother huffed. The crowd laughed.

"That's likely from what I hear about you," the judge grunted. He turned a sharp eye on the crowd, and placed a revolver on top his bible. "Is there anyone who objects to this union?"

No one dared. Not even in jest.

"No? Good. You have to say your names for the law."

"I, Isobel Saavedra Amsel take Atticus James Riot to be my partner and husband."

"And I, Atticus James Riot, take Isobel Saavedra Amsel to be my partner and wife."

"And we'll take Jin and Sarah to be our lawful daughters," Isobel added.

"Agreed," Riot said, reaching out an arm to encompass the two girls. Sarah began crying, and Jin's lip started quivering.

"That's settled," the judge said. "By the power in… Oh, rings." He waggled his hook at her.

Tobias White stepped forward, and began patting his pockets.

Miss Lily looked heavenward. Then the boy pulled out a ring tied to a string that was connected to a button on his waistcoat. There were some minutes of him trying to untie the ring, until he gave up and yanked the button free. He dropped it into Riot's waiting palm with a wide grin.

"I didn't want to lose it," Tobias whispered.

Riot winked. "Smart lad."

It was a circle of gold with an intricate wave-like pattern around the band, but far too thick for a normal ring. Before Isobel could study it overly much, Riot took her hand in his, and held the ring poised. "With this ring, I thee wed." He slipped it on her finger, then passed a gold ring to her for him.

"You still have your hat," she whispered as she slipped the ring on his finger. The edge of his lip quirked.

"Husband and wife!" the judge announced. "Now kiss her, boy."

It was a chaste kiss. Riot hadn't dared do more with Isobel's parents watching. But she didn't have such reservations. When he started to draw away, she captured his mouth with her own to cheers and hoots. Then Tim struck up a lively tune.

The next hours passed in a blur of smiles and well-wishing, of good food, and dance that would last until the sun fell to the horizon and set the ocean aflame.

Isobel swirled on the dance floor with an enthusiastic Scotsman, who practically carried her along. The jig died, and Mack roared for another, but Tim struck a slow cord, and Vicilia joined in with his guitar. Riot stepped in, offering a hand, which Isobel gladly accepted.

Riot danced a fine waltz. He led her with a gentle touch and a sure hand as he gazed into her eyes. The deck dropped away, the guests, and even the sea. There was music, and her husband, and nothing more.

"How did you manage this?" she whispered.

"A wedding at sea seemed fitting. I thought you'd like it better than a courthouse."

"I do," she said with feeling. "But a ferry?"

"It was Tim's idea. Well… a remark of his reminded me of a fellow from the seventies: Shanghai Kelly. That Irishman chartered an old paddle steamer and threw a birthday bash for himself. Free liquor and… other attractions. Kelly invited the whole of the Barbary Coast, and when ninety souls were aboard he cast off. The liquor was heavily drugged."

Isobel glanced at the wine bottles. Her father had donated his wine cellar to the occasion. She doubted it would put much of a dent in his stockpile.

"When the celebrants were passed out, Kelly pulled the steamer right up alongside the *Reefer*, a notorious hell ship in need of a crew, and unloaded his party for a small fortune."

Isobel laughed. "Good God, that's brilliant."

"I'm sure the shanghaied men didn't think so when they sobered up."

"And *that* made you think of this? So romantic, Riot. But it must have cost a fortune to charter a ferry…"

He tilted his head. "I knew the captain was fond of cards."

"You wicked man," she said.

"I never claimed to be a saint." He twirled her deftly and they danced past Jin, who was dancing with Tobias. From the dread on the boy's face it wasn't voluntary. Tobias looked like he had been taken hostage as Jin pulled him around the cabin. Riot reached over and tapped Jin on the shoulder. The girl tried to dance away, but Riot kept pace, and Isobel flowed along with him.

Riot held out his palm. "Pay up."

Jin huffed at him, and then glared at Isobel. "Only a crazy person would leave at midnight! How could you?"

Isobel clucked her tongue. "You should know better."

Jin fished in her pocket and slapped a gold coin on Riot's palm. "I did not think you were actually crazy."

"Not about that," Isobel said. "Never wager with a professional gambler, Jin. But really, Riot, *you* should know better, too."

"Know what?" he asked innocently.

"Wagering with a ten-year-old child? Your daughter?" She arched a brow at the twenty dollar piece in his palm.

"I suppose you're right," he said with a sigh. "You're in luck, Jin." He handed the coin back to her, and she beamed. Before Riot changed his mind, Jin abandoned the dance floor, leaving Tobias without a partner.

"Gah," the boy said. "I thought I was a goner."

Riot shared a look with Isobel, who smiled in return. He had never planned on keeping Jin's coin.

Wine and laughter flowed in equal portions. Children darted around the ferry playing a game of catch me if you can, and Isobel only had to pull Jin off the bulwark once when the child decided to put on a balancing act for the other children.

Eventually Isobel slipped from the din of laughter and conversation to stand at the deck's railing and watch the last rays of a dying sun. She glanced back to the cabin—through the windows to the misfits, the in-betweens, and friends, none of whom fit society's mold. They warmed her heart.

Someone came up beside her and leaned on the rail. She didn't need to look to know who it was. She could feel him. And it wasn't Riot. Her husband was inside dancing a stately waltz with her mother.

"I hope you're as worried as I am," Lotario drawled. "Mother is probably cursing him, or giving him advice on how to give her grandchildren."

Isobel snorted, and turned back to the sea. The ferry was chugging its way towards Richardson's Bay near Sausalito. "Whatever she's saying, I'm sure Riot can handle her. Sarah finally let you rest?" Lotario was a popular dance partner with the ladies.

"The reporter, Mr. Fry, saved me. I think he's besotted with her."

Isobel frowned. "Sarah's only twelve."

"Fry isn't much older. And don't forget what *you* were doing at twelve."

"Sarah isn't me. Or you, for that matter." Isobel turned to look through the window. Cameron Fry was a pale, lanky lad with a shock of blond hair, a perpetual sunburn, and a voice that tended to crack.

"If he's doing what *I* was doing at his age, then you definitely don't have to worry about your daughter."

Isobel placed the reporter between fourteen and sixteen. "He better just be after a story," she said. "Why on earth is he here?"

"An exclusive on the wedding in exchange for our approval of the article."

Fry would make a tidy sum.

Isobel gave a dismissive gesture. "That means nothing. His editor has the final say."

"His editor kept his promise when Fry interviewed Sarah."

"There is that." She turned away, confident Riot would keep an eye on the young man. "How was the *Narcissist*?"

"I didn't go there," Lotario said.

"You didn't?"

"I see Atticus didn't tell you." Lotario sounded pleased.

"No, he didn't. He was stubborn about it." Isobel looked her twin up and down, narrowing her eyes. He appeared healthy, if a little drunk. And he wore gloves. "What are you hiding under those gloves?"

"Probably the same as you."

Isobel started to reach for his hands, but he shooed her back. "You'll find out soon enough. Stop spoiling your own surprise."

"I hate surprises."

"That's only because you don't like to admit that your powers of observation aren't up to par."

"With as much wine as I've had… they definitely aren't up to par."

Lotario chuckled. "I think my friends are trying to drink father dry."

"Impossible," she said.

Lotario moved closer, putting an arm through hers, and resting his cheek on her shoulder. "What will I do now that you're settled with a man I actually approve of?" It was a flippant question, one he didn't really mean, but an idea sparked in her mind.

"Come live at Ravenwood Manor with us," she blurted out.

Lotario straightened. "One of your daughters is being put in an *attic*. There's no room for me. You know how I like my space."

"You can move into a room when there's a vacancy."

Lotario took her hands. "Bel, I need my own life."

"The offer stands, regardless."

"Thank you," he said, and meant it.

"At least come for dinner regularly."

"I will," he promised. "What are your plans?"

"My *immediate* plans?"

He waggled his brows. "We all know what that will be."

Tobias shot past them on deck. He was trailed by one of Dr. Wise's sons, and then a girl (one of Isobel's nieces), followed by Jin, hot on their heels. Jin looked about to tackle the girl. Good thing she was Emmett's daughter. His children (and wife) were as sturdy as he.

"Honestly," Isobel said when the bang of footsteps faded, "I haven't thought beyond tonight."

Lotario smiled like a cat. "That's the answer I was hoping for."

A horn blew, the paddles stopped, and the *Tiburon* bobbed on Richardson's Bay.

"Let's go starboard. I haven't given you your gift yet."

Curious, Isobel followed her twin to the starboard side, where the celebrants were gathered on deck. Masts bobbed in the night, and distant lights blazed from Sausalito's Water Street.

Riot stepped up beside her and handed her another glass of wine.

"A toast," Lotario said, raising his own glass. "To the bride and groom. To my twin. My reflection. Your happiness is mine, and the day would hardly be complete unless you sailed into what's left of the sunset." Lotario smiled at her. "My gift to you." He swept his hand towards the bay in a grand gesture, and with that signal Tim lifted a hooded lantern and shone the light on a moored boat.

Isobel was dimly aware of Riot rescuing her wine glass as it fell from her numb fingers. Her feet took her to the rail as she stared at the shape of a familiar cutter.

"It's the only way I'll ever get rid of you," Lotario drawled in her ear. It was *her* cutter, the *Pagan Lady*, polished and gleaming, and whole. "Try not to sink her again."

THE GIFT

To her credit, Isobel retained her composure through the farewells, and tolerated more hugs than she had in her entire lifetime. It was, after all, a special sort of day.

After giving Jin a laundry list of things she was not to do, Isobel handed over her daughters to their grandparents.

Catarina inclined her head to Isobel. "You're fortunate the ferry didn't sink and drown us all," her mother said by way of farewell. "I would have preferred St. Mary's Cathedral, but I'm glad you're properly married now."

"It was lovely seeing you too, Mother." Isobel's only consolation was that Catarina would have to keep watch on Jin for an undetermined amount of time. Marcus hugged her, and then grabbed his son-in-law into a typical German embrace, and then her again. Where Catarina lacked in displays of emotion, Marcus made up for in spades.

Hop took her hand warmly, and Isobel kissed him on the cheek. "I don't know who I'm more worried about, mother or Jin," she whispered. "Either way, I'm sorry."

"No one can compare to you, Wu Lei Ching." Fox spirit. It was an insult, of a sort. But he meant it fondly.

Riot helped Isobel into a dinghy, and a seaman rowed them over to the *Pagan Lady* to cheers and waves. By the time the *Tiburon* chugged towards the Sausalito ferry terminal, Isobel stood on the *Lady's* deck, exhausted. "I think I've sprained my cheeks," she admitted, exploring the injury with her fingers.

"It's fortunate I don't intend to make you smile tonight."

"*Really*?" Isobel stepped into the cockpit, inspecting the *Lady*. Lotario had replaced the tiller with a proper wheel. Freshly varnished wood gleamed: pine and oak, and a new hollowed mast of Douglas fir. "What do you intend?" she asked.

Riot glanced at the hatch. He had a calculating look about him. Moving with uncanny speed, he hopped into the cockpit, and hoisted her over a shoulder.

Isobel squeaked with surprise, then laughed, as Riot attempted to carry her below deck. It was a tight fit, and she only bumped her head twice. He set her down in the saloon, and kissed her smile. And then each burning cheek.

"You're lucky I'm too intoxicated to mind."

"I had noticed," he said, tossing his hat on a hook and shrugging out of his coat, tie, and collar.

Isobel stared at her new cabin in amazement. "Lotario must have completely gutted her." New wood, new design, everything shining in the lantern light and smelling of fresh wood and varnish. A tight pilot's desk with nooks for maps was tucked beside the galley. The double settees still lined the sides of the main cabin, but Lotario had added bunk-like shelves above the seats. For the girls, she realized. With curtains for privacy. Her gaze followed the curves and cubbies, a masterpiece of design.

"How did he manage it?" she asked, breathlessly. At some point the shock had floored her, and she realized she was sitting.

"Lotario commandeered your family's shipyards. The design and a good amount of finish work was all his doing."

Isobel glanced at her husband. He was properly disheveled in his shirtsleeves. He knelt in front of her, and started unbuttoning her shoes. Isobel let him, too exhausted and overwhelmed to deal with details. He tugged her shoes free, and his fingers drifted up her silk stockings, before slowing unrolling them. He helped her with the buttons of her gown, and finally the laces of her bodice, until she could breathe again.

Wearing only a chemise, she slid onto his lap, and his arms came around her. "*All that we see or seem is but a dream within a dream*," she quoted Poe softly.

Riot buried his nose against her neck. "I feel like I'm dreaming too. And oddly floating."

"We *are* floating, Riot."

"It may be the wine."

"Or lack of sleep."

"Or joy," he added.

"That, too."

"When did you sleep last, wife?"

That word. It sent a thrill down her spine. "Oh, I don't know. Sometime before yesterday."

Riot shifted his arms so they were under her, and stood, lifting her effortlessly. She let him, because it was one of those days, and he was that kind of man—a rare one who made her enjoy being a woman.

He carried her to the forward cabin. Lotario had changed that, too. Instead of a jumbled mess of ropes and sails, and four bunks that were never used, he had added a nook with a double bed across from the head. And a sliding door. Portholes let in air, and a hatch let them see the stars.

Riot set her down, and Isobel stretched out on the bed.

"Do you think Lotario kept the original secret compartment?" Riot asked, as he shed the remainder of his clothing. He looked on the verge of launching an investigation.

Isobel dissolved into a fit of helpless laughter.

Riot paused, and then finished folding his trousers. "Not really a reaction a man wants while disrobing."

"Oh, Riot."

He looked sheepish. "There isn't a smuggler's compartment, is there?" he finally asked.

"There *was*. After a fashion."

Riot stretched out on the bed beside her, and propped his head on a hand. She turned to him. "Do you want to guess?" Isobel asked.

"Considering I've spent a good hour searching for this famed secret compartment, I think not. I'm all out of guesses, and I'm far too tipsy."

"An hour?" she gasped. "For shame, Riot. Going through a woman's things."

"It was enlightening," he admitted.

"Just so. I'll make you work that sluggish brain. But I'll take pity on you and give you a hint—that business with Curtis and the manner of my abduction."

A light went on in his eyes, or thought returned northward. Either one, he had the answer. "The spare sail that used to be here."

"Good show, Watson!" she exclaimed. "Lotario rolled one of his lovers in it when said lover's parents sent the harbormaster to search for their son." She placed a hand on his chest. "You look disappointed."

"I really thought you two would have a smuggler's compartment."

Isobel raised herself up and looked out into the narrow corridor. "Maybe he added one? We could spend our wedding night searching."

"I wasn't planning on spending the night investigating anything but you."

"You've spent many such nights already."

"I like to be thorough."

That voice. Deep and soft all at once, it never failed to capture her. Isobel felt her cheeks warm, and to hide her blush she quickly rolled on her back to study her new ring. They weren't in any hurry after all. They had the rest of their lives together, and she was simply happy to *be* with him in that moment. "You managed a ring after all." She slipped her gold ring off. "No more new hats for you?"

"It was Ravenwood's ring. I wanted to give you a… an heirloom. Something from my family. I suppose Ravenwood is the closest I had."

Isobel turned it in her fingers, and narrowed her eyes. A wave-like pattern decorated the outer surface, and two tiny screws were set on opposite sides. As she had noted before, it was thicker than it should be. She nudged the inner layer, and gasped. Four rings within one—it opened to form a sphere with tiny numerological symbols on the bands.

"An armillary sphere!" she cried with delight. An old device that navigators used to determine the position of the sun and stars. It was a symbol of Portugal, and it represented wisdom and knowledge—a model of the universe.

"I thought it might make the universe less daunting for you."

The ring blurred in her hand. Before she gave in to the overwhelming emotion that threatened, Isobel reached for something familiar: sarcasm. "You found it, didn't you?"

"I did find it," he confirmed. "But…" Riot took the ring from her unsteady fingers and closed it, slipping it back on her finger. "I had to fight Jin and Sarah for it."

"And they took pity on you after they won?"

"Indeed."

The banter cleared her eyes. Thankfully. Her emotions had escaped from a box long ago, and she wanted to shove them back. But perhaps, for today, she'd let them have free rein. "I love it," she said with feeling. "But not as much as I love this boat." She turned to look him in the eyes. "And not near as much as I love you."

"I'm heartened to know I rank above the *Pagan Lady*."

Isobel kissed him, slowly, and his hands slid down her body, pulling her close against his own. A yawn cracked her jaw, and Riot chuckled in that silent way of his. He smiled against her lips. "Sleep first," he whispered.

As much as she hated to admit it, forty-eight hours without a wink of sleep along with an unknown amount of wine had done her in.

"We're doing things out of order again," she said.

"I can think of nothing better than waking up next to you." He tugged the quilt up, and they settled beneath it, listening to the lap of water against the hull.

Isobel snuggled into his arms, molding herself against his body. "All those months of talking sessions and relaxing baths," she murmured. "And all I needed was you."

"And your father's wine."

Isobel might have chuckled on her way to sleep, but she couldn't be sure. It was a perfect end to a perfect beginning.

If you enjoyed Uncharted Waters, and would like to see more of Bel and Riot, please consider leaving a review. Reviews help authors keep writing.

Keep up to date with the latest news, releases, and giveaways.
It's quick and easy and spam free.
Sign up to my mailing list at www.sabrinaflynn.com/news

Now available:

Book 7 of Ravenwood Mysteries
Where Cowards Tread

HISTORICAL AFTERWORD

Mainstream history tends to focus on big events. But there's a whole forgotten, or little mentioned, history that often gets overlooked—that of individuals. Especially women of color.

I first came across Mary Ellen Pleasant in a book on fantastical stories of San Francisco. It painted her as a criminal mastermind who performed Voodoo rituals on young women, so they'd seduce rich men and make Mrs. Pleasant rich. Although tantalizing from a writer's viewpoint, I was skeptical. The newspapers of the time (and still today) relished sensational news and were extremely prejudiced against non-white races. SF papers published all types of rumors about Mary Ellen Pleasant. The papers had a love/hate sort of relationship with her, and coined the derogative name 'Mammy Pleasant' for her, a name she despised but used to her advantage when needed.

When I started digging further, I found that she was shrouded in mystery. It's difficult to separate rumor from fact, but she was most definitely a shrewd businesswoman, who defied her social standing and gender to amass a fortune. She was an abolitionist who worked in the Underground Railroad, a civil rights activist, real estate magnate, entrepreneur, financier, and was even called the *Mother of Human Rights in California* for taking a case to the California Supreme Court for a ruling in her favor that outlawed segregation in the state's public transportation system.

You may be wondering about Miss Lily's hair product venture. That's based on fact, too. Two women: Annie Malone and Madam C.J. Walker saw a need for hair products made especially for African-American women. The harsh products of the era were made using ingredients like lye, which caused severe dandruff and baldness. Annie Malone became one of the first African-American women millionaires, and Madam C.J. Walker came close to it, being the wealthiest self-made woman at the time of her death in 1919. Both were philanthropists and entrepreneurs who overcame harsh prejudices against race and gender to succeed in an intolerant business world.

And for anyone wondering if such a bizarre wedding between Bel and Riot was possible in the supposedly proper year of 1900, I'll share this excerpt from the Los Angeles Herald in October of 1898:

> ***Ex-Husband the Best Man***
>
> *Baltimore, Md. —On Monday Mrs. Minnie A. Ostertag got a divorce from Albert Ostertag, on Tuesday she received a license to marry John Emmert, and last night the wedding took place over the saloon conducted by Ostertag, with the ex-husband as best man. There were many guests at the wedding. Mrs. Ostertag was dressed in her best and Emmert was in high feather. The wedding procession was unique. The musicians came first, playing a lively tune.*

Following them came two little girls with flowers, and then Ostertag, staggering under the weight of an immense wedding cake. In his wake were his divorced wife and the man she was going to wed. Ostertag advanced after the wedding and gave his ex-wife a hearty kiss, wishing her well with her new husband. Then he cried: "These people need something to drink," and went behind the bar and dispensed drinks to the guests. The neighbors say that Mrs. Emmert, who is the real owner of the saloon, agreed to keep her divorced husband in the house and give him $1 per week for his services.

Suddenly, Bel and Riot's wedding seems positively mundane. But I hope, at least, it was romantic.

ABOUT THE AUTHOR

Sabrina Flynn is the author of ***Ravenwood Mysteries*** set in Victorian San Francisco. When she's not exploring the seedy alleyways of the Barbary Coast, she dabbles in fantasy and steampunk, and has a habit of throwing herself into wild oceans and gator-infested lakes.

Although she's currently lost in South Carolina, she's lived most of her life in perpetual fog and sunshine with a rock troll and two crazy imps. She spent her youth trailing after insanity, jumping off bridges, climbing towers, and riding down waterfalls in barrels. After spending fifteen years wrestling giant hounds and battling pint-sized tigers, she now travels everywhere via watery portals leading to anywhere.

You can connect with her at any of the social media platforms below or at www.sabrinaflynn.com

Made in the USA
Coppell, TX
09 February 2022

73241526R00069